MW01193539

SEDUCTION THEORY

ALSO BY EMILY ADRIAN

Daughterhood

Everything Here Is Under Control

The Second Season

SEDUCTION THEORY

A Novel

EMILY ADRIAN

Little, Brown and Company

New York Boston London

The characters and events in this book are fictitious. Any similarity to real persons, living or dead, is coincidental and not intended by the author.

Copyright © 2025 by Emily Adrian

Hachette Book Group supports the right to free expression and the value of copyright. The purpose of copyright is to encourage writers and artists to produce the creative works that enrich our culture.

The scanning, uploading, and distribution of this book without permission is a theft of the author's intellectual property. If you would like permission to use material from the book (other than for review purposes), please contact permissions@hbgusa.com. Thank you for your support of the author's rights.

Little, Brown and Company
Hachette Book Group
1290 Avenue of the Americas, New York, NY 10104

Little, Brown and Company is a division of Hachette Book Group, Inc. The Little, Brown name and logo are trademarks of Hachette Book Group, Inc.

The publisher is not responsible for websites (or their content) that are not owned by the publisher.

Book interior design by Marie Mundaca

ISBN 9780316584517

Printed in the United States of America

For my husband

This is how a god says goodbye:
If I am in her head forever
I am in your life forever.

— Louise Glück

Then the lights go out and it's just
   the three of us
You, me, and all that stuff we're so
   scared of

— Bruce Springsteen

SEDUCTION THEORY

SEDUCTION THEORY

Roberta Green

A Thesis Submitted to
Edwards University in Partial Fulfillment
of the Requirements for the Degree of
Master of Fine Arts

Department of Creative Writing
Edwards University

CHAPTER ONE

At the creative writing department's end-of-year party, Ethan's secretary fed him kale with her fingers. Ethan wasn't supposed to call Abigail his secretary. Trouble was, Abigail often referred to herself as his secretary in wry subversion of the school's progressive values, and her jokes had eclipsed her actual job title in Ethan's memory. The party was crowded. Grad students were crammed into the kitchen, hoping their advisors heard them talking about sex. In the adjacent living room, academic spouses grew weary of discussing summer plans, as if everyone had summers off. Soon the house would overheat. Guests would spill into the yard but for now stayed close to the collapsible buffet table on which they'd placed their offerings. "I brought the kale salad," said Abigail, who was not attractive but to whom Ethan was attracted. He'd formed a habit of fixating on her least appealing features, her crusty eyelashes and fleshy earlobes, daring his lust to subside, which it did not.

"I'm not a fan of that vegetable," he admitted.

"Oh, I massaged it. Have you ever had it massaged?" She looked deep into his eyes with an intensity that might have indicated sexual devotion but was not uncommon in the type of person by whom Ethan found himself daily surrounded.

"I'm not sure. I mean, I don't know how it's usually prepared."

She stuck an arm between two adjuncts and grabbed a fistful of her own salad. She was drunk. He was excited.

Abigail shoved the greens through Ethan's closed lips. Oh, they were terrible. Coarse and curled and bitter, gritty with some kind of debris. "Are there nuts in this?" he asked.

"Quinoa."

"Ah," he said, chewing indefinitely. "That is different."

Pleased, she drank her drink. Ethan stood ass-to-ass with party host and department chair Joyce Lockhart, who was engaged in a separate conversation. "We adopted him when he was seven," Joyce was saying. "He was called Humphrey on his papers, which, no. Then we discovered he hates females his own age but loves puppies, so we named him Humbert!" Temperate laughter. Someone's sandalwood perfume. "Lola" by the Kinks.

"Do you want to smoke a cigarette?" Ethan asked Abigail. These were the first words he had spoken to his beautiful wife, Simone, when they were just shy of twenty-one. Abigail would not want to smoke a cigarette because Abigail was thirty-nine, a single mother, and wearing a scarf in June. Abigail said, "Oh!" and "Yes?"

That Abigail said yes might be the whole story.

Depending on the wind, the town smelled of turkey shit from the turkey farm or sugar from the cereal factory. The town necessitated long underwear, compost piles, one fundraiser after another. No one affiliated with Edwards would admit any fondness for the town except undergrads committed to college-town mystique. Few would claim to hate Londonville as Ethan did. His hate was a comfort, a creed. He knew who he was and where he would never belong.

Abigail sniffed the air and said, "Turkey shit." Was she not a grown-up version of the girls he'd kissed behind the bleachers at his high school in Portland, Oregon, one hundred years ago? Ethan recognized the thought as a version of what all adulterers told themselves: the affair was predestined, inevitable. Had essentially already happened. What they were doing was not an affair because Ethan had never laid a hand on Abigail. But it also was, because leaving a department potluck to buy cigarettes was better than sex.

"Tell me something," he said. It was a game. No follow-up question, but an open call for something, anything. To use the line on Abigail was not a betrayal but a test. She would falter, she would fail, proving she was not the other woman but the lesser woman.

"Oh," Abigail said. "I've never smoked a cigarette. This will be my first."

He was so happy. "Say more!"

"I've always tried to limit my vices. I drink sometimes, but that's about it. I think I'm fundamentally a bad person, like in my soul, so I don't really need the accessories."

"What makes you bad?"

"I want to punch everyone I've ever been mad at. Steal from anyone I envy. Jump into bed with anyone who pays me a compliment."

Her silence started a clock. This was his chance to say *You have a beautiful neck* or *Your posture is pristine.*

Ethan said, "I'm trying to guess your middle name."

"You'll be guessing all night."

He guessed Wendy and Crystal and Inez. She said, "No" and "Ha!" and "My middle name is Marie."

"Marie is common."

"I know, sweetie."

His blood ran warm. He held open the door to Shef's Convenience and watched Abigail go through it. Her gauzy scarf was gray or green; her gauzy dress was green or blue. These clothes were in the business of implying, not flattering. He wanted her to wear what he wanted all women to wear, what his wife wore: tight jeans and a black tank top. The style did not strike him as particular to Simone. He did not realize the extent to which he didn't know women and only knew Simone.

Beside the register was a bowl of rotten bananas and a folded index card on which an employee had scrawled *BANANAS 75 CENTS.* Ethan regarded Abigail regarding the inedible fruit—her open skepticism and repressed laughter—and wanted to lick the neck he'd failed to compliment. Instead, he selected a turquoise lighter and asked for Camels. How did he and Abigail appear to the man behind the counter? Ethan thought they might look like teenagers, wild with tension, on the edge of oblivion. The door buzzed as they left and he thought, no. They looked like what they were.

The sky performed a sunset. From his first inhale Ethan was desperate to grind the cigarette beneath his shoe. After all these years, smoking felt silly and indecent. He could barely look at his secretary, whose shallow puffs bespoke mutual regret. God, he missed his wife. Simone, tenured, had skipped the party to stay home and read. He wanted to divorce her so they could meet by chance ten years from now and do everything they'd ever done a second time.

"How's your—"

"Don't," he said.

"I was going to say book."

"I know you were. I should've been a carpenter."

"I've heard that line about a thousand times. What is it with you people and carpentry?"

"We're useless with our hands." He offered her the one without the cigarette. "Feel how soft. I've never labored!"

She touched his hand. They rounded the corner of Maple Street and encountered a small, quivering terrier.

Abigail gasped. "That's Humbert!"

"Who?" He wanted her attention to himself.

"Joyce's dog. He must've gotten out." Abigail sank to the

ground and collapsed her shoulders. She looked lopsided, sub-missive. "Come here, sweetie."

"The real Humbert Humbert loathed dogs," Ethan said.

Abigail laughed. "The real?"

Ethan decided to let this woman change him. In this moment he would be dog-friendly. He ceased looming and copied her crouch. Humbert approached, and Ethan palmed the animal's undercarriage. The terrier vibrated warmly in his arms, and the word that came to Ethan's mind was *winner*.

It was hotter inside the house than out. Perspiration shone on every forehead. Were academics sweatier than regular people? He posed this question to Simone in his mind. Ethan waited at the threshold of the party, heroically holding the dog. I saw him come in, and back then I knew him only as Simone's unworthy husband, whose fiction workshop I'd so far avoided, whose ped-agogy skewed teddy bear. He looked so proud proffering the terrier. Euphoric, enchanted even. Abigail gazed up at him, the first lady of his office of self-destruction. Was this what Simone had seen in him when she was my age?

"Humbert!" Joyce's many beaded necklaces slapped as she made her way through the crowd. Rosewater. Room-temperature pork. "These Days" by Nico. "He was supposed to be shut inside our bedroom!" Joyce looked mischievously or judgmentally or neutrally between Abigail and Ethan. "Did you let him out?"

"We found him on Maple Street," Abigail said.

"Goodness." Stroking the dog's small skull, Joyce showered him with kisses and admonishments. Ethan looked down at

Abigail. Hers was the load-bearing smile of middle age, revealing every wrinkle she would ever have.

"I'm going to exit this party soon," he said.

"Oh, yes," Abigail said. "Time for me to relieve my babysitter. I'm likely to crawl into bed with my five-year-old so I don't have to sleep alone."

"I love your honesty," he said.

"Thank you," she said. "I love that you're seven feet tall."

He was only six four.

Ethan didn't need to convince himself his wife was beautiful; she always had been, was becoming more so as they aged. Tonight she had fallen asleep with the lights on. She wore gray, university-branded sweatpants and a silk shirt half open to an expensive bralette. Strewn across Ethan's side of the bed were Virginia Woolf and James Joyce, several Cambridge Companions, and a plate smeared with ketchup. He removed the plate and stacked the books on the nightstand. Stripping down to his boxer briefs, he flipped the light switch and arranged his body against hers on the mattress. "Tell me something," he said.

He felt his wife emerge from shallow sleep. He felt her struggle to produce a compelling answer. The struggle meant something to him.

"Reviewer two fucked me over," she said.

Ethan considered himself comfortable with the ways Simone was a real professor, and he was not. She had a Yale PhD, a scholarly book with Oxford, a daunting list of publications—though her students worshipped her for a popular memoir she'd written about her mom, and for her hair.

What his wife wanted was to speculate about reviewer two's identity. The peer who had fucked Simone's article was almost certainly a close friend from her Yale cohort. Reviewer two might have been Marshall, who'd taken twelve years to write a dissertation and landed at NYU Singapore, or Mackenzie, a Wiccan who once hissed at Simone mid-seminar, "Bite your tongue!"

Ethan and Simone had fallen in love at Vassar. After graduation he moved with her to Connecticut, where he worked at a coffee shop and wrote *Muse,* the novel that qualified him for the spousal hire at Edwards. During those years in New Haven he'd contracted an outsider's inferiority complex while cultivating a sexy, edgy indifference to academia. They were married in the living room of their Wooster Square apartment amid pizza boxes. "Elvis Presley's Blues" by Gillian Welch. Metal bars on the window. Simone's vintage minidress evoked spontaneity, Las Vegas. They vowed never to lose interest in each other. Guests weren't sure if the wedding was ironic or sincere, and their gifts reflected their uncertainty. There was a cake pan shaped like Hogwarts and a set of blue martini glasses.

They decided never to have children. "I want to spend the rest of my life reading books and undressing you," Simone said, eyes welling with wine-warmed tears. What had Ethan said? What he always said to her. *Yes.*

Tonight he didn't care about reviewer two. From his wife he

craved a compliment, or some indication he was known beyond the parts of himself he advertised. For instance, she might roll over and ask, "When did you get so lonely?"

Alternatively, he would accept a piece of personal lore she'd waited until now to tell him, intuiting he would need to be reeled in from the waters of infidelity. Was she voted homecoming queen at Chappaqua High School? Did she ever stash an infant turtle in her closet until it died? *Say something funny,* he thought. *Make a little joke!*

Simone had gone back to sleep.

In the morning, the happy couple jogged into the path of their secretary. Abigail held a paper sack of groceries beneath one arm and wore linen pants cut into shorts. She had knees like the rumpled faces of newborns. Where was Byron, her five-year-old son? Maybe waiting in the car, if that was legal, or—knowing Abigail—even if it wasn't.

Did Ethan still categorize the cigarette he'd smoked with Abigail as infidelity? No. The cigarette had assumed the abstract, blameless quality of images that flashed through his mind during intercourse: Shin guards on a volleyball player. Tattooed cashier at the hardware store. He was unaware of any recklessness in his thoughts or behavior. He was aware of being a novelist who hadn't sold a book since he was twenty-six, and of a morning heat too aggressive for June, and of Simone's sweat mixing with traces of her cologne.

"Hello Abigail," Simone said. "Were you at the party last night? Did you have more fun than my husband?"

Abigail spoke into her grocery sack. "I love dogs, so."

Simone's smile was broad and genuine. Weirdos were her weakness.

"We found Joyce Lockhart's dog," Ethan explained. "Stepped outside for some air and there he was."

Ethan's embarrassment in the moment was out of proportion with what was happening. His secretary was talking to his wife. His wife was beautiful, and his secretary's neck was slick with sunscreen. Abigail asked about their plans for the summer: they were going to Oregon, the annual trip Ethan received in exchange for living in the Northeast, where people referred to anything outside as "nature." His mom, Lois, still lived in Portland, and he missed his mom. His missing Lois could not compete with Simone missing her mother, who was dead.

"Portland? I'm going there too. Middle of July," Abigail said. "Maybe we—"

Ethan laughed.

"Well."

The three of them stood on the sidewalk smiling at each other.

Jogging is foreplay. Those spandex-clad couples wearing fanny packs and shamelessly sweating outside the coffee shop, they're about to fuck. Whenever I saw Simone and Ethan out for their Saturday morning 5k—her stride short and efficient, his bouncy, uncontrolled—I would torture myself picturing what came next. She would keep her sports bra and shorts on when she straddled him. Her kink was staying partially dressed. She liked the implications, which, in her imagination, were power and urgency. Atop her husband she spread her knees, allowing him to pull the damp crotch of her shorts to one side and push his fingers into her. She cried out often and because she could. They had no roommates. No kids.

Simone found language for her orgasm. "Like skipping a stone across a pond, the stone hitting six or seven times."

"Very nice," Ethan said sincerely. "There's something I want to tell you."

"Same," Simone said. "You go first."

"I think I'm becoming friends with Abigail."

Ethan was never sure what his wife would say. Simone wasn't prone to stock phrases or detachment. She was the most alert person he'd ever met: a student of each moment of her life.

What she said was "I think that's exciting."

That his wife didn't question his need to confess his friend-ship with another woman seemed to excuse Ethan from any guilt or introspection. Did he realize it wasn't Simone's job to scrutinize his motives? No. Unthinkingly, he trusted his wife to prevent his self-destruction. He believed her judgement auto-matic and accurate—a spousal superpower.

"Men should be friends with women, because women know how to be friends," Simone said.

"Men don't?"

"Not really. Men have colleagues and tennis partners. Drinking buddies. They send each other Spotify links. If a more meaningful bond develops over the years, then maybe you tend to it. Whereas there's this woman in the history department—you've met Sandy. The first time we had coffee she showed me a picture of her stillborn baby."

Ethan felt lightheaded. If anyone showed him a picture of a dead body over coffee at Manic Mondays—amid that mess of kitsch and '90s ephemera, the damp backpacks and shrill laughter of his own students—he would pass out on the floor. "Weren't you horrified?"

Simone's contemplative habit was to watch the ceiling fan. "Sandy was trying to tell me what she had endured. That was generous, I think. She wanted me to know our friendship didn't have to be superficial."

"What did you do?"

"I cried."

"You cried at Manic Mondays?"

"We both did."

"Who would even think to take a picture? I mean, you're in the hospital and you've just suffered this terrible tragedy..."

"They send in a photographer. It's optional. It's the only picture you're going to get."

"I didn't realize you and Sandy were so close."

"She had another child since then. We've drifted apart."

"Abigail's son is five." Ethan found it stirring to imagine Abigail pregnant.

Simone said nothing. She watched the ceiling fan for a long time, and Ethan became nervous. Finally, she asked, "Why do you want to be Abigail's friend?"

His answer was unrehearsed. His answer would have been the same if his wife had asked "Why do you want to have sex with Abigail?" or "Why do you feel such tenderness for her fleshy little body?" But Simone hadn't asked those questions, and one of the profound comforts of personhood was never having to answer a question no one had asked.

"She reminds me of kids I grew up with. She reminds me of my sister, if I had one. You ever read one of those profiles of twins separated at birth, or women and the children they gave up for adoption reunited later in life? And how they can tell they're related? They do the same hand gestures or both gag on olives? Does that sound insane?"

"I had a thought," said his wife. "I've been thinking about something."

Ethan might have noticed the difference between those statements were his heart not in his throat.

"Maybe I shouldn't come to Oregon," she said.

He stroked her hair and asked, "Why don't you want to come to Oregon?"

"I want to train for a fall marathon. And I want to read *Mrs. Dalloway* with Robbie. And I don't know, I always say yes to everything—but maybe? Try this. Ask me if I'll go to Oregon with you."

Rarely, but lately, their most intimate interactions carried an air of performance. If Ethan asked himself for whom they were performing and why, he became terrified, and so he didn't.

"Simone, will you come to Oregon with me? Will you eat black bean burgers with my mother? Will you sleep on a mattress stained with my adolescent fantasies?"

As a younger man he'd dreaded separations from Simone. When she took a semester's leave from Vassar to grieve her mother and pack up her childhood home, Ethan wept himself to sleep each night. When Simone had abandoned Ethan in New Haven so she could present at conferences or interview for postdocs she didn't end up needing, he'd felt hollow and useless until the moment she returned. But they were older now. They had spent years upon years in each other's company. To part ways would not be painful but an exquisite imitation of pain, like watching a sad movie. He looked forward to sleeping in the center of a queen-sized bed — to building his wife knee by hip by shoulder in his mind. The ache would be so satisfying!

Simone said, "You know, I think I'll stay."

Ethan felt calm, or rather, elated. He enjoyed not knowing what would happen.

CHAPTER TWO

Why did it torture me?

Forgive the cliché, but the first time I saw Simone—first class, first day of graduate school—I didn't know if I wanted to sleep with her or be her. All I knew was desire simmered low in my stomach and I wanted to make something happen. I hadn't predicted these feelings when I registered for her workshop already knowing about her fifty-four thousand followers, her cheekbones, her internet feud with a Sterling Professor of Humanities at Yale, her internet friendship with the creator and star of an HBO show, the nine-hundred-dollar slip dress she wore to the National Book Awards, her ability to run a sub-six-minute mile, and her forthcoming scholarship on nonmonogamy in the twenty-first century. Honestly, all that left me cold. Then she took her place at the head of the table, regal in a sleeveless turtleneck, arms on display. Before giving us the prompt for our generative exercise, she produced two figs from her briefcase and ate them.

"Write about a time someone embarrassed you."

The course was called Memory as Narrative. For twenty minutes, in my childhood chicken scratch no amount of occupational therapy had improved, I wrote about my mother dropping me off at Smith. The shame that washed over her when she realized hers was the only daughter who hadn't brought a plastic shower caddy. Two weeks into the semester, a package arrived. A gift so large it obscured my view of whoever got on the elevator with me, tittering at the dimensions of my unwanted parcel. Inside: face masks, exfoliating scrubs, bath salts, loofahs, moisturizers, emery boards, and the triple-decker, mildew-resistant caddy to end them all. The ladies of my floor and of my ilk (Blundstones, flannel) hooted at the loot, hysterical at the idea of me, Robbie, practicing self-care.

I kept going. I wrote about the royal-blue polo shirt and matching scrunchie my mother wore chaperoning my eighth-grade field trip to the Empire State Building. The toenail fungus she never bothered to conceal at the beach. Her constant plea for book recommendations and her raw, unworldly reviews: Barry Hannah suffered from depression. Marilynne Robinson needed to get laid. I volunteered to read my piece, "Thirteen

Ways My Mother Has Embarrassed Me," out loud. Did I consider that Simone's mother was famously dead? Did I aim to console her? (Moms—bad actually!) No, I must have wanted exactly what I got: laughter from my classmates and Simone's icy silence. I watched her take in the ungroomed, uncouth spectacle of me.

"What Roberta's story needs is less Roberta."

My classmates sat up straighter, pleased to not be me.

"A virtue with which every writer should acquaint herself," Simone went on, "is humility."

She did not smile. My mortification at her hands was ecstasy.

Ethan got a good deal on a flight out of Rochester with a brief layover at JFK. Simone was more than willing to drive him to the airport. She liked to listen to the radio in their Subaru Baja and stop for sausage McMuffins. When he offered to take a taxi, she said, "Absolutely not," grateful for the chance to spend time with him before he left.

It was post-McMuffins, a half hour into the drive, when Ethan received a text from the airline. There had been a gate change. The first flight of his trip from SYR to PDX would now board at Gate 15.

Ethan lost feeling in his feet. The radio played "Stand Back" by Stevie Nicks and the corn stood high in the fields.

"I'm flying out of Syracuse," Ethan said.

"Fuck." Simone put on her turn signal. She pulled into a gas station and updated her phone with the correct address. "We lost some time, but we left the house nice and early. You'll make it."

She got back on the two-lane highway and resumed driving, faster now and more intensely engaged with the Stevie Nicks song—which was longer than it should have been, or had the DJ played it twice? She hummed the chorus. Simone wasn't mad, not even annoyed. Something Ethan admired in his wife was her precise sense of when she was suffering and when she was not. Rarely did she seem aggrieved.

Ethan wanted to cry. It wasn't the extra minutes in the car or the possibility of missing his flight but his failure to anticipate the mistake he would make. Why hadn't he checked? He was confident his flight was from Rochester; he often flew from Rochester. He could have sworn he remembered the subject line in his inbox: *Check in now for your flight from Rochester!*

Simone reached across the gearshift and took his hand. "We weren't even driving in the wrong direction. It wasn't the most efficient route, but it wasn't wrong."

"I'm sorry." Like most apologies, his was self-indulgent.

"Don't be." Simone checked her mirrors for cops, then accelerated. They arrived at Syracuse an hour before takeoff. Their goodbye kiss was prolonged and European. His mistake would slip promptly from their minds and have no bearing on any future story they told about Ethan, their marriage, or this particular summer.

* * *

Ethan's first night in Oregon, dinner was cheese enchiladas with sauce from an Old El Paso can, served with rice and refried beans. It was the meal he wanted when his heart was broken, after a long day of jury duty, and at his funeral. His mother wore plastic clogs and used a threadbare dish towel as a napkin. They took turns describing episodes of podcasts they had listened to while walking in the rain. Ethan respected Lois, could not yet imagine a time when his respect would be eclipsed by a bewildering combination of compassion and resentment.

They stayed up late watching a PBS documentary about the eruption of Mount St. Helens. As the credits rolled, Lois asked him, "Will you see any friends while you're in town?" The question confused Ethan, then overwhelmed him. Friends? Here? He didn't have any friends in Portland.

But if not here, where?

He went to bed and couldn't sleep. Had he ever had a friend? Ethan thought of Adam Shiver sliding toward a soccer ball in seventh grade, how Adam had sat up in the grass and blinked at his buckled, broken arm. Ethan said to another kid, Phil Harmon, "Bet you twenty bucks it's broken."

"Dude," Phil said, and he shook his head. Instantly Ethan understood his comment as heartless, a wager made by a sociopath, and was ashamed.

In high school Adam and Phil both played varsity, and Ethan was cut from JV. He pierced his ears and acquired a wood-paneled minivan. Stashing the back seat in the garage gave him and Caroline room to roll around. Caroline lived in a suburb fifteen minutes south of Portland and took TriMet bus 35 to a private school downtown. Ethan first met her waiting in line for the Ferris wheel at the Rose Festival. He was alone, she with an odd number of friends. "Ride with me," he begged. "I'm scared of heights." He wasn't. Ethan and Caroline broke up before college, and the narrative on which they settled was it was hard, so hard to say goodbye, because they were *best friends.* What did they mean? They meant Pavement at the Crystal Ballroom and dinner at the twenty-four-hour Hotcake and Steak House. They meant cigarettes smoked leaning over the Vista Bridge guardrail before the suicide-prevention netting went up. They meant making out. They meant marijuana. All they meant was adolescence had been fun and they'd shared it. Ethan hadn't contacted Caroline since the day he laid eyes on Simone.

In college he had four friends. His friends all looked like acoustic Bob Dylan and went by nicknames: Chubs (skinny), Fitz (last name Fitzgerald), Smokey the Beard (self-explanatory), and Philoctetes (sprained his ankle once). Nicknames never stuck to Ethan, who by that point in his life was distinguished by height and handsomeness. Smokey was the friend Ethan liked best and with whom he shared an off-campus apartment sophomore and junior years before moving in with Simone. Ethan and Smokey watched Criterion films on VHS and got high from a vaporizer Smokey, né Arthur, built in the bathroom. Their most intimate conversation concerned suicide.

Whether either of them was capable of it. Ethan could never remember who had posed the question and often wondered, because Arthur—who in the late nineties had declared himself constitutionally incapable of self-harm—took his own life two days after Ethan's wedding. Ethan hadn't seen Chubs, Fitz, or Philoctetes since the funeral.

In New Haven, Ethan declined party invitations from the baristas and dishwashers at his work. He avoided lunches with Vassar classmates passing through town. Simone's grad school friends were fleeting, fair-weather, fiercely competitive. Their main flaws, vanity and insecurity, Ethan now recognized as his own and as symptoms of youth—though at the time, he and Simone had loved to pick apart her friends' characters and find them lacking. Now Ethan had colleagues. He liked most of them, trusted none. Thirteen years ago, as a new hire, he became close with a student whose fiction was better than his. A devotee of his office hours, she grew comfortable. She told him her stories were autobiographical, including the one about her dad and the one about her childhood eating disorder. Ethan had thought of Adele as a friend—or a future friend, waiting patiently in the wings. He fantasized she would win a National Book Award and he would attend the ceremony, chastely, as her plus-one.

That same semester, a different undergrad accused a different writing professor of grooming her for sex. Ethan's panic was instantaneous. Did Adele believe he was grooming her? Was she grooming him to groom her? For sex?

25

The university's investigation of the other professor was scandalous and prolonged. Desperately, Ethan wanted Adele to stop knocking on his office door twice weekly, stop linking him to her distressingly personal blog. But how could he ask her to stop without incriminating himself? A man could not slam on the brakes of a car everyone agreed was parked. The other professor was shamed in the *New York Times*. Ethan's anxiety sent him into Simone's arms, sobbing over a mistake he hadn't made or come close to making but one that, in a world where young women were categorically imperiled by old men, could be made for him. Simone had soothed him: "There's no parallel to be drawn here. You've been good to that girl. You're an exceptional teacher."

But Ethan was not exceptional, and neither was Adele. Turned out Adele was a little bit nuts. In her cap and gown that spring, she found Ethan in his, which time had rendered a humiliating costume. She placed her hand flat against his chest and—within view if not earshot of everyone on campus—told him, "My answer would be yes."

Too flustered to be flattered, Ethan took a step back and said, "No, no, no." He left the reception early, repelled by the child's faith in her youth, her conviction her sexuality stood a chance against Ethan's beautiful wife, his three-year renewable contract, his self-respect. Later, he understood the moment as a young person's experiment. The girl was under the influence of graduation euphoria. The only question she needed answered was *Who am I now?*

Later, Ethan did feel flattered. Adele was very pretty. She was not his friend.

On the other side of the wall, his mother snored at the precise volume she'd always snored. Ethan's childhood sheets were linen and cleaner than anything in his own house. What was wrong with him? Several times, in the margin of a student's story, Ethan had written, "Why is this character always alone?"

Loners were convenient in literature, of course.

His brothers were his friends! Brian and Jasper came in through the back door without knocking. They wore puffy vests over flannel shirts, shorts. Their beards were untrimmed and multicolored. They hugged Ethan so hard he worried for his skeleton. His brothers asked zero questions about his work, wife, or home life. Brian and Jasper drank three cups of black coffee each and said, "Remember when we broke your nose and you cried?"

"Remember when we found seventies porn behind the Franz bread factory and you saw too much pubic hair and cried?"

"Remember when Mom crashed the car merging onto 205 and you cried?"

Ethan's brother Brian was on an SSRI for his anxiety. Ethan's brother Jasper had stopped drinking six beers per night for his anxiety.

"Do you have anxiety?" Brian asked Ethan. "Does it run in the family?"

"Yes," Ethan said.

"What do you do for it?" Jasper asked.

"Cry," Ethan said. His brothers howled with laughter, they loved him so. Their mom brewed more coffee and cleaned the sink with a smiling sponge called Scrub Daddy. Brian imagined Scrub Daddy as a kind of pervert and Jasper objected, vehemently. The sponge was a father figure. A self-respecting man. Ethan enjoyed the intensity of his brothers' debate. Behind teal-rimmed drugstore glasses, Lois rolled her eyes.

Jasper said, "Hey Mom, hey Mama, who's your favorite son?"

Lois smiled as if recalling the best vacation of her life. "Simone."

Brian and Jasper booed. They too had wives who could have been contenders. Wives who went pheasant hunting with them in the fall, raised their children, and on feral summer evenings challenged each other to underwater breath-holding contests, barefoot races across the yard. When present and called upon, Simone would participate—placidly, and with no desire to win. The first time he watched his wife attempt to play, Ethan understood Simone had never been a child but a patient passenger of her youth.

"We're kidding," Jasper said. "Simone is the right answer."

"You outkicked your coverage," Brian said.

"What does that mean?" Lois remained willfully ignorant of the sports that had colonized her backyard and television in the 1980s.

"He doesn't deserve her," Jasper said.

* * *

I feel weird about the Adele part, and I want to clarify a few things. Ethan's perspective was flawed. The car was not in park. From Adele's point of view, the car was in second or third gear, meaning Ethan had given his student reason to think he would welcome her palm flat against his chest. Reason to believe the question she answered had actually been asked. Yes, she told him about her violent dad and starving herself in high school, but only after Ethan cleared his throat and said, "Sometimes fiction feels true to life, and sometimes it feels truer than life, and in rare instances it's both."

He held her gaze while she told him which parts of her stories had really happened. His office door was closed when he said, "You're breaking my heart."

Not only did he fantasize about an evening as Adele's guest at the National Book Awards, he told her, "When you win a prize for your debut novel, I want to be there. I don't care if I have to rent a tux."

He was aware of having said things he shouldn't have. He imagined Simone overhearing and asking for a divorce, and Ethan vacillated between telling himself divorce would be a grave overreaction and believing, in his bones, Simone ought to dump his ass.

After the incident at graduation, Ethan came clean to his wife. He told Simone about Adele's hand on his chest. He revealed that his anxiety during the investigation of the other professor had also been guilt; parallels existed. He no longer remembered which lines he'd toed or crossed or dreamed of crossing. Had he said or only thought the thing about being her chaste plus-one? Did he rest a hairy, predatory hand on her knee while she showed him the calorie-counting app to which she'd briefly been enslaved? Perhaps he couldn't trust himself to know the difference between a student and a mistress, a silly girl and his wife.

His wife: "And when she propositioned you at graduation, how did you respond?"

"I shut it down! I cried out as if burned!"

Of this he was certain. He came close to admitting he'd had a crush on his student, and that he'd encouraged the one she had on him, but Simone didn't force an admission.

What was a crush, to Simone? In her view, desire was built into education. Why else would the pupil obey her instructor? Personal pedagogy aside, Simone's feelings were hurt. She was disturbed by her husband's recklessness and naivete. And she forgave him in a week, which was two days longer than it took Ethan to forgive himself.

Adele was not nuts, and I want to resist going out of my way to depict Ethan as decent. He's married to Simone, of whom I'm inclined to think the world. I don't want anyone to think so poorly of Ethan they think less of Simone for loving him. Maybe I'm complicating something simple. Maybe it's enough to say that Simone was brilliant, her beauty was unimpeachable, and good women marry the wrong man all the time.

* * *

Ethan had been in Oregon two weeks when Simone asked him to have phone sex. She called in the morning as he was pulling on his jeans and searching a pile of soiled laundry for his wallet. Living with his mother made him slovenly. Midnight EST would work best for Simone, phone-sex-wise. She had evening plans to see a movie with a friend. Who was the friend? Ethan failed to wonder.

"I'm meeting Abigail at the park today," he said.

"Oh, a playdate," Simone joked.

Ethan had told Abigail where he was staying, and she'd suggested Wallace Park. He envisioned the two of them walking downtown or into the West Hills, perhaps stopping for coffee. Today he would ask his secretary if she'd ever broken a bone and why she kept a picture of Roger Federer taped to her computer monitor but never mentioned sport. In Ethan's mind, these questions were devoid of romantic energy. These questions were all business. As he approached the park, he evaluated his posture reflected in car windows and made an effort to straighten his spine. His heart rate spiked, either in anticipation of seeing Abigail or of phone sex with his wife. He wasn't sure.

This three-week trip would be the longest he and Simone had been separated since the second semester of their junior year. During Simone's absence from Vassar they'd had zero phone sex. Truthfully, in college they'd been nearly too inept to have regular sex. Both did their best but felt betrayed by eros, which seemed to require math. Ethan and Simone couldn't get their angles right. They found themselves crunching numbers in their heads. They enjoyed the negative spaces before and after sex more than they enjoyed copulation itself. Things had since changed.

At the edge of the basketball court stood Abigail in train-conductor overalls. Beside her was a small child with a fresh buzz cut. Based on height alone, Ethan would have guessed the child was three.

"Are you Ethan?" the boy asked fluently. "Do you have a job?"

Simone hadn't been joking when she said *playdate.* As usual, she'd been trying to tell Ethan what was about to happen.

Ethan sank into a squat. "I work at Edwards with your mom." It was ten in the morning and the kid smelled of grass and rancid yogurt. "I'm a professor."

"Okay," the boy said distantly, as if Ethan had spoken at inappropriate length. "Do you sleep with any animals or do you sleep alone?"

Ethan avoided looking at Abigail as he said, "I usually sleep with my wife. What's your name?"

The child made a sound Ethan could not interpret.

"Byron," Abigail supplied.

Byron said, "You know what I feel like doing? I feel like swinging for a while." Without athleticism he sprinted for a swing set across the soccer field. Ethan stood and his knees sonically cracked.

"Byron's learning to pump his legs." Abigail straddled the

bench of a picnic table. "He'll want to be alone while he practices." She smelled faintly musty, as if her overalls had been left in the washer too long. Beneath the overalls she wore a tight sports bra that pushed rolls of fat toward her armpits.

He sat beside her. "Remind me — what's your connection to Portland?" He'd already forgotten the questions he'd planned to ask.

"My father moved here after my mother died. He lives with a woman he met on the internet. What about you?"

"My mom lives a few blocks from here. Same house I grew up in."

"Is your dad still alive?"

"He's alive in Tampa. They've been divorced since I was Byron's age."

"You're lucky she's single. I fully cannot deal with my father's girlfriend. She's ugly and smug and won't let Byron eat popcorn on the couch. What we should do is hatch a scheme wherein my father and your mother fall in love."

"Goodness," Ethan said.

"That would make us stepsiblings." Abigail nodded once.

"How strange," Ethan said, adoring her.

Abigail kept her gaze fixed on Byron, who pumped his legs so aggressively the whole swing set groaned and trembled. "I shouldn't be so hard on Diane. It's just that every time we visit I'm shocked all over again. She's always here and she's never my mom."

"Simone lost her mother young. Right after we met, actually."

"I've read the book." She might have meant Simone's memoir or Ethan's novel. The books were essentially the same. "Simone intimidates me."

There seemed to be a maternal advantage in never being expected to look away from your offspring. Excused from eye contact, a person could say outlandish things.

"Why?" he asked.

"Why does someone so smart need to be so sexy?"

About Simone, Ethan had often wondered the same thing. As the most acclaimed scholar in their department, Simone could have opted out of silk shirts, skintight jeans, those little heeled boots. She could have let her muscles go slack, her waistline soft with middle age. Her face could have sagged into Arendt levels of androgyny and no one would have respected her less. Instead, Simone was a campus sex icon. Her author photo occupied the entire back cover of her memoir.

A perk of being married to Simone was Ethan's certainty that the best sex of his life lay ahead of him. After college their skills improved gradually until a point in their mid-thirties when Simone underwent a fundamental shift. Ethan never knew if it was throwing out her birth control pills, or the success of her first nonacademic book, or if her stubborn, full-bodied grief had finally dissipated. Simone had become unselfconscious and insatiable in bed. When Ethan asked about the change, Simone sat up against a mound of pillows, long hair netting her breasts, and said, "I've fallen deeper in love."

"I'm hungry." Byron had returned. "I need a snack right now."

Abigail was already rummaging through a white tote bag with dirty straps. "What would you like, sweetie?"

"Goldfish, celery, strawberries, cheese, chocolate milk."

To Ethan's astonishment, Abigail produced each of these items. She arranged four small containers and a yellow thermos on the picnic table.

"A martini, a prime rib, and a baked potato," Ethan said.

"What?" Byron's mouth sprayed cracker crumbs.

"A little joke," Ethan said.

"But jokes are funny," Byron countered.

"Ideally, yes," Ethan said. "Some fail."

"I'm lost." Abigail looked up from the depths of the tote. "Is your family going out to dinner?"

"No." A swell of optimism inspired Ethan to touch her back. Her skin was freckled and hot. "We should have dinner while you're in town."

Abigail became ecstatic: she had a habit of bookmarking restaurant reviews. She was most desperate to try a place on Division Street that combined Thai influences and American soul food. Would he like to meet her there next week? Her father and Diane could babysit.

"Yes," Ethan said.

He followed her to the edge of the park. As she buckled Byron into his car seat, Abigail spoke excessively about car seats. Children these days had to ride in a booster until they were nine or ten. There were many variations corresponding to the child's weight and height. Most airlines would check a car seat for free, but the thing was still a pain in the ass to travel with. Ethan enjoyed her monologue, more or less. As an academic he had willingly lost hours of his life to dinner-party lectures on tick-borne illnesses and whether a poet could write a novel more or less easily than a novelist could write a poem.

Abigail clicked the last buckle and shut the door of her father's maroon Buick. She introduced Ethan to a new kind of hug. Soft arms above her head elongated her torso. She encircled his neck and applied the full length of her upper body to his. Leaving space between their pelvises meant pressing their chests together firmly, encouraging her ass to stick out high and round.

He liked her the way she was—dank overalls, sockless feet swelling in tight canvas shoes. He liked her, and while he loathed himself for liking her, loathing did not extinguish the pleasure of liking. Their hug was interminable.

"Take care of yourself," Abigail said. "You seem a little sad."

He hadn't realized he was sad.

Simone began by describing the underthings she had ordered from a boutique in New York. The bra was wireless and sheer. Simone's brown nipples strained against the lace cups that could, in a moment of agony, be instantly unclasped from the front. The matching thong was irrelevant. Simone had removed it. And now her ink-stained fingers traveled the length of her taut abdomen, down through the hollow of her hips. She stroked her dense, flattened hair and parted her labia, labia that had caused Ethan to gasp out loud on his twenty-first birthday. Before that night, their first together, he hadn't known the softness of snow and heat of August commingled between the legs of the woman he loved.

"You're hard," she said into the phone.

"Yes."

Afterward they stayed on the line and regulated their breathing. Ethan was sober but felt hot and disoriented, ageless. Simone was a fantasy conjured from his childhood room, the original dream factory. He missed her so much.

Their conversation diluted itself. They moved from "I love you" to acknowledging the farce of phone sex to Simone asking Ethan about his day.

"It was fine. Nothing special."

"How long were you with Abigail?"

"An hour or two. Her kid was weird but cute."

"Abigail is weird but cute."

"There's something—" Ethan was aware of having a motive and unaware of what it was. "There's something stunted about her. Maybe about all moms? As if there's a limit to how much you can grow as a person once you've made a person."

Simone was silent. Ethan imagined her gaze on the ceiling fan. He often felt overwhelmed by the statistical unlikelihood of inhabiting any particular moment of his life. Why should this happen now rather than before or after? What difference did the present make? Simone called these episodes "Ethanian attacks." Now was not the time to admit to having one.

"That's insane, Ethan. She's been through things we can't imagine. Our lives involve nothing approaching that level of responsibility. We're the ones for whom growth is limited."

He was never able to predict when Simone would side with another woman over him. Her sporadic allegiance to her sex always took him by surprise.

Ethan, age forty-one, was eating eggs off his favorite rooster plate when his mother said, "Book club tonight. We meet on the porch at seven thirty."

Ethan said, "I'll make myself scarce."

"Well, no. Our book this month was *Muse,* and the ladies have questions for you."

Ethan held a piece of toast between his plate and his mouth. Simone would be upset to have missed this.

"Don't look so aggrieved," Lois said. "It's a matter of convenience. We try to read local so we can host a Q and A session with the author."

The questions would be: Where do you get your ideas? Do you write at the same time every day? Tips for combating writer's block? Did you aways want to be a writer or did you plan to be a firefighter, major-league pitcher, ballerina, optometrist?

Ethan hadn't admitted he wanted to be a writer until

college. In the Oregon of his youth, young men did not wear Dockers, did not read Roth or Bellow, and when tasked with transporting assignments home shoved their papers loose into their backpacks—volcanoes of unwashed socks, orange peels, bottle caps. Ethan kept secret his habit of reading four novels a week, along with his total reliance on narrative to make sense of his otherwise arbitrary life. It had been a relief to arrive at Vassar and discover his roommate shelving the complete stories of Flannery O'Connor, Faulkner's novels, everything Melville ever wrote. Yet the stuffy self-seriousness of the Northeast would also oppress him. The rejection of pretension meant something to Ethan. So did recreational recklessness. *Such a boy,* his mother had often said about all three of hers. It was Ethan, more than his butch brothers, who still cherished the characterization.

Muse was the book he wrote while Simone was in grad school. Not autobiographical but biographical of his wife. Simone had lost her mother when she was twenty, which was two years too late to be treated as an orphan or, it turned out, with much sympathy at all. After six years earning between ten and twelve dollars an hour pulling espresso shots for Yale undergrads, Ethan was paid $250,000 for the novelization of Simone's debilitating grief. There was a rave *New York Times* review, an appearance on a national morning show, emails from peripheral friends paranoid that Ethan had become famous, modest sales, and no second book. Not because he hadn't written a second (and a third and a fourth) but because his first had not, in the end, been worth the price of a five-bedroom single-family home in Indiana. Publishers had never forgiven him their miscalculation.

Officially, Ethan was at peace with the trajectory of his career. As a lecturer at Edwards he was ineligible for tenure; no one cared if he published or perished. His novel had been a dream come true because Simone had read it, loved it, and loved him a little bit more for writing it. The reason he secretly, desperately wanted to publish another book was simple. At forty-one he was a better writer than he'd been at twenty-six. He wanted people, including those to whom he wasn't married, to notice.

The women assembled on his mother's screened-in porch in a splendor of earth-toned linen. They wore enormous glasses and Grecian sandals laced up their spotted ankles. They shouldered *New Yorker* or Powell's tote bags and cradled copies of his book adorned with fluorescent USED stickers. Where had Lois found these women? Lois had worked as a nurse from ages twenty-two to sixty-five. Ethan had only known his mother to read mass-market mysteries and memoirs by medical professionals.

Ethan was wrong about the questions, which were:

"How did you find your agent?"

"What is your agent's email address?"

"What was the amount of your advance in US dollars?"

"Was the book optioned for film and television?"

"Did you work alone or with a ghostwriter/freelance editor?"

"Are you available to ghostwrite/freelance edit the novels of others?"

"What is your hourly rate in US dollars?"

Ethan panicked as if onstage, as if perched on a perilous stool before a microphone, as if his answers would be uploaded to a nonprofit's YouTube page. He fumbled definitions of *query letter* and *royalty statement*. He said, "I don't consider myself a novelist anymore, not primarily. I'm more of a professor. My wife and I are on faculty at Edwards University—in upstate New York? We find teaching very rewarding."

The woman seated closest to his mother pressed her copy of *Muse* to her chest. It was the paperback cover a publicist had assured Ethan was "Oprah bait" (no nibbles). The cover showed a girl from behind, standing in a loose dress, gripping her left wrist in her right hand. "Is your wife here?" the woman asked. "We'd love to meet her."

"Simone is darling," Lois said, "but prolific. She stayed home to work."

Ethan excused himself. He climbed the creaking, curving stairs to his childhood room and flopped upon the mattress. Through the open window he could hear his mother's book club mocking his fragility. This room made him want to get high or masturbate. Or to never do those things again. Last summer, Ethan had written an erotic historical novel about spouse-swapping archaeologists in mid-century Greece. It was based on a real-life married couple who met a grisly end. The truth was, Simone had rewritten most of the erotic parts. They rewrote each other's work all the time. Life was meant to be stolen; plagiarism was a form of love.

Working on the book, provisionally titled *Erastai,* Ethan had forgotten he was a man who'd never been to Europe. He took a break from writing and went for a jog and—lost in contemplation of the protagonist's bisexuality—tripped on a slanted slab of sidewalk, fracturing his femur. Twenty-four hours later he was entombed in an MRI scanner, arms crossed, feet hog-tied, magnets whirring and hammering while Kurt Cobain warbled through hospital-issued headphones. (He'd selected satellite station number 34: *Lithium.*) Defeating claustrophobia, Ethan had closed his eyes and plotted his next chapter.

What he most wanted from writing was that feeling of immersion. The process always felt like self-effacement—though the end result, he knew, was indecent exposure. He wanted to be taken seriously, to be known as a serious writer. And he was a man whose hands still craved the texture and heft of certain sports equipment; he also wanted to win.

As the women on the porch below asked his mother if Ethan had always been *sensitive,* Ethan threw open his laptop. He wrote an email to his agent—not his original agent, who had forsaken him, but his original agent's son.

Can we try ERASTAI again?

Before dinner with Abigail, Ethan shaved his face, the perimeters of his ears, and the coarse hairs that sprouted sporadically from his shoulders. It would be unfair of me to equate grooming with intention. Don't we often aim to look our best for those with whom we have no prayer of sleeping? Individuals whose generous visions of our naked bodies will never be corrected? But the fact remains that Ethan shaved his ears before his date with his secretary, and I do want to present the facts as I understand them.

Of his lust, Ethan was fully aware. He was counting on rigorous, teasing conversation. If moved to do so, he would press his knees against Abigail's beneath the table. He probably wouldn't, but if it came to that, he would permit himself the pleasure. At least once they would sustain soulful, electrifying eye contact communicating unspeakable depths of—something. Saying goodbye on the sidewalk outside the restaurant, Abigail would formulate an approximation of a question: *In another life?*

She'd flatten a soft palm against his chest. That would be okay, just this once. And he'd answer, "In a heartbeat," the way he couldn't to Adele. She could tell him to take care of himself; he'd liked that the first time. And back in Londonville their friendship would continue unscathed, a private homage to what might have been.

Key to his fantasy was Ethan keeping the dinner a secret from Simone. She was his life's witness. Since they were twenty years old he had confessed to her his every transgression, whether it concerned their wedding vows or not. To Simone he would remain categorically loyal, if slightly less accountable. Was it wrong to court some glimmer of a private life? Was it a crime to want to be wanted?

He got to the restaurant five minutes early, and Abigail was already there. The restaurant was crowded, so cramped he worried she wouldn't want to push back her chair to stand and hug him. But she did. She wore something he knew was called a sundress, though he didn't know how he knew; Simone would never wear one. Abigail also wore what Ethan considered too much makeup—meaning enough for Ethan to notice it was there. Twice the server attempted to take their order before either had glanced at the menu. Finally they ordered, family style and at random. Abigail may have quickly ruled out personal allergens and dishes that disgusted her. Ethan didn't bother. The food was very good.

"Tell me your life story," he said.

"I'm from Boise."

He gulped wine. "That makes sense."

"Getting into Edwards was the best moment of my life. Not something you're supposed to say as a mother, but."

Ethan hung on her every word.

"Childbirth is torture for women, and falling in love with your child—well, that's also a kind of torture. I think most people, if they're honest, can trace the best and worst moments of their lives to particular emails or phone calls. Don't you?"

He disagreed. He nodded.

"So I majored in English literature"—she pronounced every syllable, presumably in defiance of the Potato State—"and got the admin job right after graduation. I meant to move on from the job and from Londonville, but hello health insurance! Hello gorges! And suddenly then I was thirty. There was an older grad student studying Russian lit; I don't know if you remember Victor? He and I were off and on for the better part of a decade. He would move in with me and change his clothes seven times a day. The man produced unholy amounts of laundry. I still haven't recovered. He wanted me to come to the city and I couldn't go. I don't know if it was Victor or Brooklyn, but I was pathologically incapable of committing. We were together when I got pregnant and broken up again by the time Byron was born. I figured having a baby together bought us a few more reunions, but no. He takes Byron for two weeks in August. That's the most we see of him."

Beneath the table, Ethan pressed his knees against hers. They both flinched at the sound of a woman who was not their server clearing her throat. The woman was tall, wide-hipped, long-haired, Mormon.

"I'm so sorry. I saw you and had to know. Did you write a novel called *Muse*?"

Mute, Ethan nodded.

"That book got me through a tough time." The woman was repeatedly jostled by irritated waitstaff. She stood her ground. Waving tightly at Abigail, she asked, "Is this your wife?"

"Colleague," Ethan said.

"Oh." She was mournful, and Ethan knew he'd lost a fan. "Nice to meet you both." No names had been exchanged. The woman squeezed her way back to her table.

Now came the sustained eye contact between Ethan and Abigail, more embarrassing than electrifying.

"Happen a lot?" Abigail asked.

"Never in my life."

"I bet it happens to your famous wife."

He was distracted by the rhyme. Life/wife. Wife/life. White lie.

"The thing about Simone," he began, his nervous system desperate to stop him, "is she's brilliant. But she's fundamentally stunted in some way. I'm not sure if childless women develop past a certain point. Their lives aren't challenging enough."

Abigail sat back in her chair. She lifted her wineglass to her lips. Her wrist bones were notably elegant.

"You're not wrong," she said.

I want to be clear about two things. In this moment, Ethan betrayed his wife. He did so completely and with his hands in his lap. Correctly he had sensed his love of Simone was a roadblock in his pursuit of Abigail—not because he was married to Simone, but because Abigail didn't like Simone. Ethan's devotion to a woman Abigail found smug and pretentious was off-putting. Was he stupid? Did he not see people for who they were? To prove he hadn't been bewitched by Simone's radiance, Ethan needed to admit a spousal flaw. And because he couldn't think of any, he invented a flaw to flatter the one virtue Abigail possessed that Simone lacked: hardscrabble maternity.

Another thing I want to emphasize is Ethan's belief in his own free will. He thought it was his decision to risk a marriage that had never been anything but safe, stable, deeply rewarding. As he paid the bill in cash, he noted with sadness he'd lost his mind. What a shame! What he didn't know was how aggressively, how specifically, a woman as sidelined as Abigail wants to defeat a woman as celebrated as Simone. What he never could have guessed was the extent to which this was all my fault. (It's ten p.m.: do you know where your grad students are?)

Ethan had walked to the restaurant. Now he rode in Abigail's car to the suburb south of Portland where her father lived. Did he notice she had styled her sundress with a pair of Crocs? He did not. He was astonished to realize it was the same town his high school girlfriend Caroline came from. The coincidence soothed him. In Ethan's mind, there remained a chance his actions were inconsequential. Juvenile. He anticipated a basement with wall-to-wall carpeting and a pool table. They would get high and listen to Low. He would not tell his wife. He and Simone were still young, too young to punish each other for every dumb mistake. They had no children; life was long. He loved her as much tonight as he ever had. No. More. It was his unwavering love for his wife that enabled him to feel such tender pity for his secretary, and to be unthreatened by that tenderness.

There was no basement. Abigail's father lived in a pink ranch house near the Willamette River. The front door was flanked by two bear cubs carved from driftwood. For the first time in his life, Ethan had sex without saying "I love you."

CHAPTER THREE

On the second Monday of my first semester, I redeemed myself by showing up at Simone's office, wanting her to sign my copy of *Motherless.*

A lock of hair had escaped the braid I'd slept on. I smelled like the cafeteria's marinara sauce and deodorant reapplied midday. In the hall, the department secretary loudly wondered to an unseen office mate if she should have her child evaluated for ADHD.

"Come in," Simone said, moving aside her laptop and a mug of tepid coffee. "I'm happy to sign your book. Let me find a pen that's not dead."

"Your memoir is the reason I applied to Edwards," I

confessed. "You're one of my favorite writers working in the hybrid genre space."

No, that's wrong.

On the second Monday of my first semester, I redeemed myself by showing up at Simone's office, wanting her to sign my copy of *Motherless*.

My hair was brushed into a clean ponytail, revealing the perfect shells of my small ears. I smelled like name-brand laundry detergent. In the hall, the department secretary loudly wondered to an unseen office mate if Professor Charlotte Stevenson would ever bother to collect her mail.

"Come in," Simone said, standing up from her swivel chair. "It would be my pleasure."

"Your memoir is the reason I applied to Edwards," I confessed. "You're one of my favorite living writers."

"Ominous." Simone mimed slitting her own throat.

On the second Monday of my first semester, I redeemed myself by showing up at Simone's office, wanting her to sign my copy of *Motherless*.

I was svelte and without sleeves, Simone style. I smelled like rosewater. In the hall, the department secretary loudly wondered to an unseen office mate if anyone would ever want her sexually.

"Come in," Simone said, smiling at her best student, who would one day win the awards for which Simone had been shortlisted. "I've been hoping you'd stop by."

"Your memoir is the reason I applied to Edwards," I confessed. "I'm in love with you."

Absolutely not.

How about this? On the second Monday of my first semester, I asked Simone to sign a copy of *Motherless*—which I'd purchased from the campus bookstore and finally skimmed the night before—as an obvious pretense for showing up at her office.

I wore something I thought Simone would like; I licked a finger and smoothed my eyebrows before knocking on the open door. My heart beat absurdly, and I knew if Simone complimented any aspect of my life or person I would be happy, truly happy, for a period of three to four days. One difference between a girl in her early twenties and a married woman who just turned forty is I can recognize a crush when I have one. In the hall, Abigail said something about despising her ex.

"Come in," Simone said.

"Your memoir is the reason I applied to Edwards." I had

applied to ten fully funded programs. "You're one of my favorite living writers."

My copies of the books that seduced me into graduate school were water-warped, spine-cracked, smeared with ink. Simone must have noticed my edition of *Motherless* was barely touched. Oh well. There was no need to go overboard. My goal wasn't to beguile her. What I wanted, standing before my professor's desk, hole in my tights, was to offer myself. I was there, I was smitten. I was hers for the taking.

"*Living* is an underrated adjective," Simone said, "and one that does not apply to this pen." She searched her desk for an alternative. I seized my opportunity.

"I'm sorry for what I wrote on the first day." When she didn't react, I added, "My in-class exercise."

"What was it?" Simone had located a Sharpie. On the title page, she crossed out her name. "Maybe I'm the one who should apologize. I don't remember."

I couldn't tell if she was lying. "About my mom thinking I would want all those toiletries?"

On Simone's desk, between a stapler and a framed picture of Ethan climbing a mountain, was a container of fresh figs. I'd never had one. "Students forget this," Simone said, passing me the autographed book, "but by the time you get to campus, I'm familiar with your work. I read your application, Robbie. I chose you."

At what point did puppy love become real?

Simone said, "Your writing is very, very good. That doesn't mean it's good enough."

"I want to be better."

She nodded. "Give me two years."

By the end of fall semester, we were in a secret two-woman book club. We read *To the Lighthouse* and *Ulysses* and *The Trial* and discussed them over Thursday night coffee. By the end of spring semester, we were training to run a marathon together— arguably the most out-of-character thing I've ever done. Typically I'm ashamed to sweat in the presence of my loved ones—and I mean that metaphorically as well as literally. For other people I aim to perform, not practice. Anything I call a first draft is my third. But Simone had given me a little speech about resisting the feminine urge to separate the body from the mind. Men closed business deals on golf courses. They challenged the new post-doc to a tennis match. They whipped wet towels at one another's butts in the locker room, and that was normal. "Let's be physical together," Simone implored me. "Let's push ourselves beyond what's comfortable."

The day of Ethan and Abigail's playdate in the park was the morning Simone and I ran sixteen miles. Having never run more than ten, I was nervous I'd fail in front of her—roll my ankle or puke or pass out on the dirt path encircling the lake. No. I got stronger with every mile. I felt like a pro. It became easier and easier to breathe in the swampy upstate heat. Simone smacked my shoulder hard to kill a mosquito and said, "Sorry to abuse you." We talked about Barthes, the necessity of seducing the reader. By the end, our strides were synced, and I felt like a loose, limber animal, the opposite of a grad student.

We finished our run at noon. Simone invited me back to her house to shower. I said yes automatically and with real joy in my heart. It didn't occur to me she was playing it fast and loose with her career or marriage. I had no understanding of her career/marriage as categorically precarious. For one thing, Simone had tenure. Furthermore, what the fuck was marriage anyway? It seemed like a game anyone in their right mind would be sick and tired of playing by now.

The living room was dark and airless and smelled like cats they didn't have. Books avalanched from the shelf and dominated every surface. Simone sat on an overstuffed couch to unlace her Nikes. She pulled her phone from the side pocket of her shorts and hit stop on an audio recording.

I figured it was a mistake her phone had made. "Was that on the whole time?" I stood in a slant of sunlight, dust swirling around my head.

"I'm lucky it didn't run out of battery."

My voice rose to an embarrassing octave. "Wait, what? You recorded us running?"

Simone said, "I love the way your brain works out there. You say things you'd never say in class or even in your work. But I get all doped up on endorphins and forget half of it. So I thought I'd try taping us."

Tape as a verb was endearingly retro. She peeled off her socks and stuffed them in her shoes. As she leaned back against the couch her abdominal muscles shimmered and flexed. I thought she was probably insane and that insanity was the price of genius.

"Will you send me the file?" I asked.

"Sure," she said. "Remind me if I forget."

I used her salon-quality shampoo and purple loofah. I changed into the outfit she offered me: a loose black dress. No underwear. I combed my hair away from my face and emerged pink-skinned, raw, younger than before. Simone, still sweating, was telling Ethan she'd call him back after the movie.

She hung up and I said, "Movie?" I was disappointed she had plans, no matter how many hours from now.

"The theater in town is showing *Who's Afraid of Virginia Woolf?* Want to come?"

I said yes. My joy knew no bounds. All I wanted was to be near her.

We spent the day together. Simone showed me her home office at the top of the stairs, decorated with framed portraits of Handsome Dan, Dame Iris Murdoch, Joan Baez—who had driven Simone's mother to Mexico for an abortion in 1969—and for some reason Freud. She told me I could use her office anytime. "You must have roommates," she said. "Or noisy neighbors."

Going to the movies felt weird. I didn't know her habits. Popcorn? Butter? Whispered conversation or respectful silence during previews? Pee at a boring part or hold it until the credits? We made it through on two Diet Cokes and a prayer. My advisor kept her hands to herself and frequently mouthed the actors' lines. She would've done well on TikTok—not that she knew how or why, and not that I planned on soiling her Gen X austerity with my Zoomer nonsense. The movie ended late, close to midnight. We'd been in each other's company for more than twelve hours, and Simone seemed suddenly anxious to get rid of me. I gave her directions to my apartment (I lived alone), and she drove erratically, too fast in the dark.

"I'm sorry!" She slammed on the brakes to avoid running a stop sign. All at once, the tension left her body. Simone laughed at what she was about to say. "Ethan and I made a plan to have phone sex. I don't want to be late."

This was a trick of hers, one I would come to understand as a classic Simonian tactic. In performing her bottomless appetite for her spouse, who was not me, she ostensibly pushed me away. But in telling me she'd be touching herself within seven minutes, well. She invited me to use my imagination. The contradiction was clear. I believed I knew what she wanted.

Deploying her marriage as a vehicle for our own intimacy: two could play that game. Two days later, we ran again. Again, I went home with her. In her sweltering office I toiled over my short story collection, the quality of which was dog shit. *Shit of the Dog* by Roberta Green: a thesis submitted to Edwards University. In the evening I accepted the first three gin and tonics she offered me.

"How did you meet Ethan?" I asked. We were toes-touching on the couch. We were sweating along with the cocktails in our hands. We had learned to show our calf muscles no mercy.

"We were at a party in someone's dorm room. In a good story, you only ever need three details to depict a party: something someone said, a smell, and a song that played. At the party, Ethan's roommate Arthur predicted Bob Dylan winning the Nobel. In the nineties all dormitories smelled like cannabis and toast. The song was "Stephanie Says." Ethan asked if I wanted to step outside for a cigarette. Neither of us knew my mother was already dying of small-cell lung cancer. We fell in love the old-fashioned way, meaning we believed we invented the concept. Truthfully, I feel the same today."

"About Ethan?"

Simone flexed her feet and grinned wickedly. (Sorry for "grin." Sorry for "wickedly.") "Yes, about Ethan. And you? Tell me your life story."

I complied. I rambled like a lunatic for an hour. Thing is, I've had an unremarkable life. I grew up in a small town in New England, the only daughter of a copywriter and a quality-control officer for the local sanitation department. As a toddler I was hospitalized for a bad case of RSV; my mother still gets anxious in waiting rooms. The winter I was thirteen my father left us for his childhood sweetheart, and in the spring my mother took him back, permanently losing my respect. I knew I was gay the moment boy-Taylor P. felt me up over my soccer jersey and all I could think about was Taylor K., girl-Taylor, girl-everything. When I got into Smith, I shrieked with certainty that my life was beginning, but I picked the wrong major. Psychology. Get real. Applying to the MFA program at Edwards was my second try, an attempted reboot. Was I finally living what could reasonably be called my life?

If the book sells, maybe.

If you find yourself enthralled by these details, you may be in love with me. Simone was. Enthralled, I mean. While Ethan ruined his life in Portland, Simone workshopped my bio. She didn't believe in killing your darlings; she didn't trust her students to know what our darlings were. Her method was to trim the fat. She cut my brother. She cut theater camp. She cut the night I went home with a bartender to see what a dick tasted like but panicked after spraying myself in the face with an attachable bidet and left through the bathroom window. (On second thought, she put that one back in.) We cut family vacations and failed tests and my first relationship.

We cut every friend I've ever had.

I walked home alone. Sometimes I think, of all Simone's transgressions, letting me out her front door that night—borrowed dress, again no underwear—would most radicalize a jury. Flirt all you want, but don't intoxicate a child and send her drunkenly into that good night! Then again, I was not a child. Women of twenty-three wander, amazed at our lightness and glee, all the damn time. "Text me when you get home so I know you're not dismembered in a ditch," we say.

All Simone said was "I'll see you tomorrow."

Notice it was not a question.

* * *

By the end of that week, I wasn't just wearing her clothes, wasn't just leaving my notes and chargers and coffee cups strewn around her office. I was sleeping on the couch and adopting her habits as my own. At dawn, we ran. At home, red-faced and sweat-slicked, we wrote down ideas gestated on the run, recorded through the Lycra of Simone's short shorts. We showered when the ideas had settled—though it was acceptable, encouraged even, if seized by a thought or annotation, to leap from the spray and drip puddles of water on the floor. We didn't eat until two or three in the afternoon, at which point we fed like animals or boys, ransacking cupboards and cramming fistfuls of tortilla chips into the mechanisms of our mouths. The hour at which we pushed aside our laptops and commenced drinking varied wildly. As early as four or, if Simone was on a tear, as late as never.

Our second to last night together, Simone got sloppy. I don't mean drunk. If anything, she seemed sober compared to me, and I wondered if she'd been decanting her drink into mine when I wasn't paying attention.

"I wish I could write about us." She shoved her knee into my knee.

"You can write anything you want."

"I'm a memoirist. I don't do fiction."

"So you can *remember* anything you want." I felt clever, exceedingly lovable.

"I don't want to write about what we've done. I want to—

what do novelists do? Invent alternative yet truer versions of true stories?"

"Stories can be true?" I closed one eye and looked at her through my blue martini glass. Simone slapped the knee of mine she'd recently propositioned. She said, "Get some sleep, Roberta."

Without leaving the couch, I got some. Had Simone called me anything other than my Christian name, I suppose I'd have followed her to bed.

The next morning, post-run. Our last day together before Ethan's return. Imagine the stillness of a house with no one's husband in it. See the window perpetually cracked because their shitty bathroom had no ventilation. Hear the cicadas outside the window. Simone's long hairs were invisible against the black floor tiles but reappeared, coiled, against each white one. I peeled off my shorts and freed myself from my sports bra. Don't dwell on the nudity of the graduate student; me naked is not the point.

I had been in the shower two minutes tops, shampooed but not conditioned, and was inspecting Simone's pink plastic razor, wondering from which of her body parts came these particular shavings, when the curtain slithered open. Here were her body parts. All of them.

"My turn. You're taking too long," said my advisor.

I looked at her nipples automatically. Her nipples were nut brown and two different sizes. Simone stood on the bath mat with her arms at her sides, and I got the sense she expected me to grade her. On what? On the enduring softness of her belly below the taut abdominal muscles she trained so vainly (but not in vain!)? On the gap between her thighs, through which the inner corners of her butt cheeks shyly touched? Her figure lacked certain markers of age and womanhood: no C-section scar, no botanical tattoos.

Should this be more unstable? A touch surreal? Simone stood naked but for her waterproof Garmin. She had forgotten to stop recording our run, and now the wristwatch advertised the fluctuations of her heart rate, which hovered below seventy, even now. Behind her, the mirror fogged over. An ice cream truck idled in the street, blasting an instrumental version of "Wonderwall." Sometimes I thought I should drop out of grad school and get a job at the bank. Gone were any misgivings I'd ever had.

What was there to say, that I would die for her? Simone already knew the depth of my devotion, the texture of my loyalty, the texture of my—

The longer I looked without touching, the more precisely I understood. She meant for me to see what I saw, and to like it. For reasons she would never admit to anyone, least of all me, her life depended on my seeing and on my liking.

"Seriously," she said, giving the curtain a shake. "Before the hot water runs out."

* * *

That night threatened to bleed into morning with no conversation, no companionship. No couch. I came down from the attic around two and found Simone reading *Humboldt's Gift*—which, believe me, was relevant neither to her academic book-in-progress nor to her three to four half-written articles nor to the collection of poetry she planned to publish under a pen name. I was furious. Ethan was re-becoming real to me. My gaze kept snagging on pictures of the two of them framed and hung in startling places. Above the bathroom mirror. In the back of the pantry. Taking in their crooked smiles, their crinkled eyes, the years having indeed run like rabbits (years that would have found me elementary, if not infantile). I wanted to cry. How could I love this woman? Why did I need her? What was she going to do to me?

I took the advice she dispensed in class and *made something happen.*

"We're wasting our last night," I said, arms crossed in the doorway.

Simone closed Bellow and laid the book to rest on her chest. "Our last night of what?"

"Of hanging out by ourselves?" I contradict myself. Who was ever more childlike than me at twenty-three?

"Do you imagine I'm only spending time with you because my husband is out of town? What kind of person would that make me?"

"I'm not an idiot."

"Robbie, you can still come over next week. And the week

after." Simone thought I'd never call her bluff. "I'd like nothing more than to introduce my two favorite people."

I rolled my eyes. "We'll meet regardless. I'm in Ethan's fall workshop."

"I'm glad. You'll get a lot out of it. My husband and I have very different pedagogical approaches."

The word *pedagogical* brought my own hysteria into focus, as she must have known it would. I felt ridiculous in the Yale sweatpants that belonged on Simone's body, a body I'd now seen. "I'm sorry. I feel" — knuckling hot tears from my eyes, I fell back on the age-old alibi of women in love — "like I'm about to get my period."

Simone's smile was maternal. "We must be synced. I'm sorry I've been aloof. You're right, Robbie. I won't have as much time to spend on you after Ethan gets home. Certainly, if I'm to remain your advisor, we can't be friends next semester. Not like this. I hope I haven't overstepped. My aim was to make your life easier, not harder. Will you stay the night again?" She sat up. Bellow fell.

It felt heterosexual, how thoroughly I'd been cucked.

"I'll sleep on the couch," I theorized.

"Enough of the couch. That couch is older than you are. We bought it at a garage sale in Connecticut. The bed is plenty big. We'll make it a slumber party."

I slept in an old T-shirt advertising a brewery in Portland. Lucky Labrador. I used a toothbrush Ethan had left behind. I was chaste and self-contained, curled up on the boy-side of the mattress. There was no question of anything happening, nary a fantasy of Simone reaching for me in the night. Her stunt in the shower had been the opposite of an invitation, I realized. What seemed, fleetingly, like naked need or true vulnerability had been a demonstration of how profoundly Simone remained in control; there were no circumstances, none, under which she wouldn't resist me.

Simone said, "You get to a certain age and start to imagine you've made your last best friend."

My heart like a hunted rabbit. "Oh yeah?"

On the outskirts of sleep, she murmured, "It's never the case."

I left early in the morning. A rest day, Simone claimed. No need to run ourselves ragged. She couldn't find Ethan's itinerary and wasn't sure when to expect him. She didn't want him to know she'd lost his email with his flight details — my first clue they did, in fact, deceive each other. I got home and changed into my own clothes, ate a bowl of granola on the fire escape because it was, objectively, breakfast time. My phone shivered with a message from Simone. She had finally sent me the audio files from our runs, beginning with the sixteen-miler.

Nothing I'd said, in staccato bursts between heavy breaths, merited preservation, but I sounded smart enough. I held my own in conversation. Mostly I liked the excited lilt of Simone's voice. Our feet clomping on the dirt path. The moments we slipped into silent, athletic camaraderie.

I was about to turn it off when I heard myself say, "Should it always be framed as a seduction? Maybe it's the grad student in me, but I think I want to be challenged more than seduced."

The muffled, clandestine quality of our voices recorded through the fabric of Simone's shorts implied a third party. Some pervert eavesdropping.

"Robbie, they're the same thing."

CHAPTER FOUR

Ethan had gone into Simone's email, deleted his original itinerary, and emptied the trash. The red-eyes from Portland to Minneapolis to Syracuse were his best option after realizing—in swampy, postcoital horror—he and Abigail were booked on the same flight home. Sex was one thing, but sharing an armrest, allowing her little hand to find his during turbulence, syncing their in-flight entertainment so they could laugh torpidly at the same moments? Ethan was not without a moral compass. He took a cab from the airport and got home at nine in the morning, before Simone expected even a phone call. Now, instead of letting him slip into the sleep of the doomed, his wife insisted on getting coffee.

"We can catch up," she said, delighted by his early arrival. Why wouldn't she be? At the kitchen sink she stood hydrating after a long, solitary run, her hair in a smooth, tight ponytail and her ass in smoother, tighter spandex. "Caffeinated, you'll power through."

"Yes," Ethan said through his misery.

They walked into town holding hands, the humidity a pretext for Ethan's sweaty palms. Aggressively his thoughts seesawed between two possibilities. First was that momentary lapses in fidelity were common and forgivable; he and Simone would still die in each other's arms as originally planned. Alternatively, this was the last time he would ever touch his wife.

The coffee shop was busy. The smell was sunscreen and compost. The song was "Running Up That Hill." Waiting in line, Simone pulled on her foot to stretch her nervous left quad. She'd been overtraining. A man at the cream and sugar station struggled to secure a plastic lid to his paper cup. The man wore a polo shirt, had one and a half chins. Ethan would have bet on the man being over fifty. But he would not have bet much; and on a second look, a squint, Ethan might have decided the man was his own age.

In fact, the man was a handsome forty-seven, a mere thirteen years older than the woman now tapping Ethan's shoulder with dispassionate confidence. "Hi, Professor."

The milk steamer whirred. The line crept forward. Adele was all grown up.

Ethan avoided the deep V of her slip dress and the hard knobs of her tanned shoulders. Looking her in the eye was an obligation and a nuisance. There had been a semester when looking her in the eye was the highlight of each week.

"I'm on a book tour for *Everything There and Nothing Here*." Adele seemed sure he would recognize the title of her novel. Not a chance, babe; Ethan hadn't googled his student in years.

"Great title," Simone lied.

The old man challenged by lids took his place beside Adele. He rested a hand on her back. Did Ethan imagine he was meeting the father of the woman with whom he'd soft-launched his infidelity?

"Meet my husband," Adele said. "Spencer, this is Ethan, my favorite professor from undergrad. Honey, I promise you you're meeting a genius. This man got me totally hooked on creative writing." Adele rolled her eyes joyfully. "Spencer calls it creative *lying*."

Ethan and Spencer smiled at each other with bland hatred. Ethan's panic in this moment had little to do with adult Adele, novelist to watch, or anything he'd felt or feared feeling a decade ago. Adele had been a child intent on making mischief while the mischief-making was good. Deep down, he approved of her tenacity. He was charmed to have been targeted by the likes of her. Ethan didn't believe she'd ever wanted to fuck him truly. In reality, people rarely wanted to fuck each other—and when they did, they did. Adele was nothing to him, except the source of an old marital conflict. Would Simone want to relitigate old wounds?

"That's cute," Simone said.

Spencer shook off the coffee dripping down his forearm. The barista blew at her bangs beneath her visor, enraged at the four of them for holding up the line. Ethan said, "Good luck with the launch."

Adele fluttered her fingers over her shoulder as she and her husband went away. The word suspended in Ethan's mind was *fool*. He and his beautiful wife got their drinks and made it halfway down the block before Simone stopped and gripped his arm. This was not out of character. Bursting with sudden insight or confession was what Simone did, and she did not select her moments with care. Morning sun burning her face, delivery truck beeping in reverse, spousal jet lag—these conditions were as good as any.

"I know I overreacted all those years ago. It was unfair of me to begrudge you a tiny crush. Half my students are in love with me and I don't hate it."

"Yes," Ethan said. But *had* she overreacted? He didn't trust his memory of the nonaffair.

"I want you to know I'm not a jealous wife. I don't expect you to go the rest of our lives without feeling close to other people."

She knows, he thought with a surge of exultation. *She knows and has forgiven me!*

"Just don't fuck anyone," she added.

* * *

The next choice Ethan made might seem outrageous—and when I first heard about it, I was horrified (and delighted, for the plot). But knowing Ethan as I do now, it's no mystery to me: Abigail asked him to babysit, and Ethan said yes.

He'd been home two days and in that time had successfully avoided his secretary. With his wife he'd had sex twice. When they weren't entwined, Ethan's anxiety spiked. Physical space between them reminded Ethan he could lose Simone and had, maybe, by his own hand (mouth, dick) guaranteed he would. What did Ethan say when Simone asked why his hands trembled? Why he kept sucking in air like a woman in labor? Why he was reading the same page of *Pnin*—his comfort novel—over and over? He said he missed his mom. The American West. His large brothers. He told these lies easily because they were true.

He was alone in the kitchen when his phone rang. He had no intention of blocking her number. He believed cutting her out of his life would be an obvious admission of guilt. Besides, Ethan liked Abigail.

She was frazzled. "I'm so sorry to ask this, but Victor was supposed to get into town today, so I scheduled an appointment—and now he's decided to postpone his trip and take Byron next week. If I miss this appointment, I'll have to wait months for another. Could you maybe...?"

Ethan didn't know about moms. He gathered you weren't supposed to fuck one and then refuse to help out in an emergency. He asked for her address, said he'd be right over. He aimed not to punish himself but to negate himself. This same urge had cost him hours of his adolescence, lost to Nintendo in friends' partially finished basements. The urge still donated small sums of money to his robustly endowed alma mater, sent him flying cross-country to academic conferences in Kansas City or Phoenix. Something he and Simone shared when they met was this proclivity for saying yes. Nurtured by marriage, the proclivity had become doctrine. Yes was their religion, and how they warded off death.

Simone, returning from her run, offered to help him babysit.

"No, no," he said. "Enjoy your shower. Byron is independent for his age." He had no idea if this was true. "I'll be fine." An equally dubious claim.

"Okay," Simone said. "Two months until race day."

He smiled at her. Ethan never thought about our marathon.

Walking to Abigail's, he indulged in self-delusion. He pretended to convince himself it was possible Simone wouldn't find out about the affair—and that it was a possibility worth gambling on, because living with his guilt was vastly preferable to living without Simone.

His plan was not faultless. He knew his marriage would be compromised by his private torment. Abigail might reveal the affair to Simone at any time—as might anyone in whom Abigail happened to confide, including department chair Joyce Lockhart or Professor Charlotte Stevenson, the four-foot-eleven trauma scholar who made herself receptive to disclosures. Byron might cross paths with Simone and say, "Mommy and Ethan

had a sleepover at Grandpa's house!" Ethan himself was a lia-
bility. The guilt could have its way with him next time he was
plastered, or coming out of general anesthesia.

Mentally, Ethan attached himself to a polygraph and allowed
a sinister test administrator to ask him, "Professor, are you full
of shit?"

"Yes," Ethan answered with a steady heart. And yet, he was
a man. At war with his intellect was a deep, mollifying sense he
could control what happened. He would not tell Simone, and
most likely Abigail wouldn't either. These were odds with which
Ethan was almost comfortable.

He wore his shorts with the five-inch inseam that made him
feel like Larry Bird. He hoped Abigail would say "Nice shorts."
His first choice would have been never seeing Abigail again, but
his second choice was to enjoy seeing her. That his first choice
was practically attainable never crossed Ethan's mind. Simone
knew and approved of his friendship with Abigail—what would
she think of its abrupt end? It didn't occur to Ethan that an
ill-advised, sexless intimacy with his secretary would probably
fizzle out. Much of what happened in Ethan's life that summer
he failed to see clearly.

Abigail lived six blocks away on a broad, leafy street hum-
ming with cicadas. The house had two front doors and two
doorbells. Because Abigail hadn't told him which to ring, Ethan
guessed. Through a frosted window he saw the blurred shape of
her clomping down the stairs. He took an academic pleasure in
having guessed correctly.

She threw open the door and thanked him three times. Her dirty-blond curls were gathered on her head in a fantastically complicated knot from which Simone's sleek hair would have instantly slipped. She showed him to her upstairs apartment. Two wiry little dogs barked without rising from the couch where they flanked Byron, his chin sagging toward a tablet.

Abigail grabbed her purse and left faster than Ethan expected. The kiss she landed on his cheek was inappropriately routine. "I'll be gone two hours," she said. "At most." (She would be gone three; after her appointment she would pull into a nearby playground, order a Nestlé Drumstick from Mister Softee, and sit in her car licking laterally, hypnotized by traffic on Highway 13. She would think *This is better than sex.*)

Byron powered off his tablet and slipped it beneath the couch. Having trusted the screen to captivate the child indefinitely, Ethan was stumped. It was all he knew about children, their hopeless addiction to the screen. "Can you do me a favor?" Byron patted the half-cushion of space between him and a dog. "Can you show me a picture of a dead person?"

An easy question. Ethan said no.

The situation escalated. Byron's tone became unbearably shrill. "Please do it! Please show me a picture of a dead person!"

"They don't really have those. I mean, no one takes those. It wouldn't be respectful."

"What's respectful?"

"It means polite. It means caring about the dead person and their loved ones. Death makes people sad."

"Show me a picture of a dead squirrel, then."

Ethan conceded. On his phone he scrolled through photos of roadkill. Byron climbed into Ethan's lap. His elbow dug into Ethan's thigh, and his hair smelled like an overly ripe peach. After thirty seconds of reverent silence, Byron whispered, "Are you sad?"

Ethan put his phone away. "A little."

"Why does everything living die?" Byron was still whispering.

"Are you worried about someone dying?"

"I won't. Never, ever."

"Has your mom been feeling okay?"

"Why are you asking me that?"

An oppressive, sticky boredom descended on Ethan. It was a sensation he'd almost forgotten, but now he remembered his grandfather's living room, baseball perpetually on the television, frozen lasagna always in the oven, never done. Ethan and his brothers resented one another for having been born. Who could love all three of them? It was an impossible task. Byron wanted a snack. Strawberries. It pained Ethan to rummage through his secretary's refrigerator, moving aside salad dressings marketed to self-loathing women, but he did it. He did it wrong. The berries ought to have been halved, as well as de-stemmed, and Ethan's negligence revealed to Byron he'd been abandoned by his father and now his mother too. She'd left him in the care of a man who couldn't be bothered to compare the width of a berry to a child's trachea; life was a lion's den. Unholy pit of serpents. Byron's screams became catastrophic. "Do you do this often?"

Ethan asked, wondering if Abigail could be evicted. He worried if he was a landlord he'd be the kind to evict a tenant for this.

"Why are you asking me that?" Byron wailed.

Ethan held helplessly on to the bowl of berries. He made eye contact with an unfazed terrier and understood the animal had a soul.

The screaming turned tearful. Instinctually Ethan knew crying was the final phase; crying signaled acceptance. "When Mommy gets home, she'll do my strawberries correctly," Byron reasoned. "While I'm waiting for Mommy, you'll get me a Popsicle. You can reach them."

Ethan could. The Popsicle dripped onto the Candyland board. "Don't win," Byron cautioned as Ethan's blue man advanced toward the Candy Castle. "Only kids are allowed to win." Ethan dutifully lost. They played Trouble and Operation and Chutes and Ladders. Why so many chutes? Between each game, Ethan reminded Byron of the tablet beneath the couch, and Byron said, "I want to play with *you*," his innocence irreproachable.

Ethan told the child he couldn't dance due to a track-and-field injury sustained in high school (in truth, he couldn't dance due to shame). There came a second tantrum. A dog scratched and whined at the apartment door. Something about the dog was familiar. A character in Ethan's youth had owned a similar breed. "Dance!" Byron shrieked as if casting a spell. "Shake your booty!" Sex was not worth this. Sex was worth almost nothing.

Heaving a sigh, Abigail merged onto the highway. In the

months following Byron's birth, no one had helped her. It was a full year before Byron occasionally slept through the night. Postpartum depression still hovered at the edges of her consciousness. She arrived home to find the pieces of every board game she owned souped together on the living room rug. Dog piss in the kitchen. Men were often useless.

"Clean bill of health?" Ethan asked. Cancer would eclipse infidelity. Thoughts were just thoughts.

Byron wrapped his arms around his mother's legs, then retrieved the tablet and disappeared into his room.

"We'll see," Abigail said, drawing out her vowels mysteriously. "I've had reasons to be extra vigilant about my health lately."

"Doctor kept you waiting a while."

"No, they were quick. I stopped for an ice cream on the way home." Her smile implied co-conspiracy. Simone would be appalled. She believed Ethan was a man of whom people often took advantage. "How did Byron do?"

"There were a few tears," Ethan admitted. "My fault."

"You've seen me naked, so I'll be honest with you. I've been hanging him upside down."

He was charmed by her, he was repulsed by her. The back-and-forth smelled like sexism. Did he, deep down, believe women were ridiculous?

"He throws these fits," Abigail continued, "and they don't stop. I try to ignore him, but he gets violent. He kicked a hole in his bedroom door—I don't even own the door! Someone screams at you that long and it affects you chemically. Adrenaline is cruel to mothers. Fight or flight, fight or flight—both are illegal! So instead I grab him by the legs. He's fifty pounds, but for now I can still grab him. And I hang him upside down. And after a minute of wretched screaming and trying to curl his torso upward like a bodybuilder, he stops."

Ethan cleared his throat. "Is that an approved method?"

"I'm not in my right mind when I do it."

Abigail portrayed as long-suffering single mother was Ethan's weakness. In general, the suffering of women struck him as deeply erotic. Simone's total unwillingness to be battered by life was, in his view, a missed opportunity. If he were a woman, he would luxuriate in his imperilment a little. Ethan didn't know he thought any of this.

At long last, Abigail said, "I like your shorts."

Ethan flexed one calf as a joke. "I was hoping you would."

"More of your thigh than I'm used to seeing—not that I'm complaining."

Could friendship eclipse infidelity? Suppose sex never happened again and they were friends for decades. Suppose Abigail married another man and the two couples drank wine in each other's backyards, vacationed together, joked about sexual tension flowing in all directions. Suppose one of the four did catch cancer and fight honorably and survive. Or die! Suppose time marched on, and Ethan and Simone kept loving each other, and at the end of the marathon of their marriage they both silently forgave the other's unspeakable mistakes.

Knowing another person better than yourself was a myth.
You could live to be a hundred, spend eighty of those years with
the same woman, and never be privy to all her white lies or dirty
dreams. Two people could agree to find that beautiful, couldn't
they? Two people could accept each other as disgraceful, dis-
honest, capable of immense harm to themselves and to others—
and that could be beautiful.

Ethan wanted to write himself into a future where Simone had
already forgiven him. To be stuck in the week he cheated on her
was the worst pain of his life. His task now was to communicate
to Abigail that they could never have sex again. He believed it was
possible to do this in a way that made Abigail feel fine or even good.

"I wonder if you can forgive me," he said.

"Forgive you?" Kindness liquefied her features. "I'm awfully
fond of you."

"Likewise," Ethan said. "I'm glad you're my friend."

"God, me too. I didn't realize how badly I needed a friend."

There had been a time when his crush on Abigail felt so powerful, action seemed inevitable. The force of his pleasure when
she walked by his desk and said "Hey, Professor"—flippant
like a student, sweet like a child—recalled his last experience
with scalding joy at the sound of his name in a woman's mouth.
Ethan had been helpless against his love for Simone. He couldn't
have stopped wanting her if he'd tried. The beginnings of the
two relationships had not been dissimilar. Did twin beginnings
demand twin ends? He didn't want the answer to be yes, but
that old dog in him had answered *yes.*

Poor Ethan. He was inexperienced. He didn't realize the ingredients of a dumb crush can mimic the recipe for true love. What he'd done with Abigail had not needed doing. The thought of leaving Simone—his only friend—to start a new life with the department secretary disgusted him, but in some dungeon of his mind he'd accepted the decision as made, cosmically, the moment he laid eyes on her.

Now he saw how miserable he would be with Abigail, whose vulnerability was an additional mistress—clingy, needy, faultless. He didn't want to stepfather a neurodivergent child. Or clean up after her dogs—except, he realized, she only had one dog. The other, the floor-pisser, was Joyce Lockhart's dog, Humbert. Abigail was pet sitting, and Ethan couldn't be bothered to remember the lives he had saved.

She planted a hand on his chest and kissed him. He pulled away.

"I'll wait." Abigail spoke so neutrally, Ethan thought he'd misheard.

"Pardon?"

"For you to realize what's possible."

His lips itched horribly. The sensation, familiar, brought on a surge of panic. "Did you eat nuts recently?"

She grinned. "On my ice cream! Naughty, I know."

The county hospital was seven miles away. Home was several blocks. Home was where Simone kept his EpiPen, which she replaced every year. It touched him, her preparedness. Her willingness to jam a needle into the meat of his thigh.

His new priority was hiding his life-threatening nut allergy from Abigail. A crisis of this magnitude was a gift he could not offer her.

"I have to go," he said.

"Please don't," she said. "Honestly, we should have a conversation. I would benefit from a real conversation."

One tainted kiss wasn't enough to induce anaphylactic shock. Ethan knew this. He also knew, with his every brain cell, the longer he stood in Abigail's living room that smelled like feet, the more damage he did to his life. "We'll talk," he lied. "Right now, I have to go."

Ethan left his secretary's apartment with little sense of how profoundly he'd failed to disabuse her of the certainty they would fuck again soon.

He wasn't proud of how badly he needed sex. Thing was, sex made a fool of plot. Sex obliterated cause as well as effect. In bed, not only had Ethan never hurt Simone, he never would. No past, no future. Nothing to regret or dread. The feeling lasted twenty minutes tops.

Ethan understood there could come a time when making Simone come at all times would seem, in hindsight, a violation. He wasn't fucking in good faith. He adored, required, and cherished his wife more than ever. Was newly recommitted to worshipping her all his days. But he was fucking a woman who didn't know he had fucked someone else, and there wasn't an honorable bone in his body.

Two days after Abigail's appointment, Simone sent Ethan into the attic in pursuit of her good vibrator.

"What makes it good?" Ethan asked.

"It's called a clit sucker."

"What's it doing in your office?" He was radiant with sweat. A patch of hair on his left thigh was curdled with semen. A fear of reproduction had recently returned.

"Internet works best up there." Simone lay belly-down on the mattress. The sheets were on the floor.

Ethan climbed the stairs, steep wooden ankle-breakers, and stood dazed in the ovenly heat. Splayed paperbacks buried Simone's keyboard. An army of mugs and water glasses guarded the window. Intermittently, an oscillating fan disturbed a slim manuscript printed in a showy font. Beside the student's thesis was a black-and-white marbled composition notebook. Ethan opened the notebook to a random page. In unfamiliar handwriting, in smudged blue ink:

They don't realize it's a balance beam.

Fear or reverence tightened Ethan's bowels. The fan blew hot air across his naked abdomen. He located the vibrator and went back downstairs. Whether tossing the notebook onto the bed was a question or an accusation, Ethan wasn't sure. He was scared and he was hopeful.

Simone lifted her head. "Must be Robbie's. She borrowed

my office while you were in Portland. Her apartment doesn't inspire."

Simone mentioned her latest mentee two or three times per day, which seemed normal. Ethan mentioned Abigail as frequently to mimic normality. He understood Simone regarded the two friendships as analogous summertime pet projects, though he believed the analogy was made in error. Ethan liked the idea of Robbie holed up in Simone's home office. Simone's celebrity status on campus was sexy to him. He loved her so much. He pawed at her breasts and whispered in her ear while she made herself come with the clit sucker.

And then his phone rang. The area code was 212, and he almost let it go to voicemail. Every writer knows the way to get what you want is to strenuously deny you ever will. New York City was only two hundred miles away, but his agent('s son) reached him from the shores of another world.

"We have an offer on the horny archaeologists," he said. "Welcome back."

Department chair Joyce Lockhart began setting up at four, though guests weren't invited to her house until eight. From the closet beneath the stairs she hauled the collapsible tables, which she would festoon with mismatched HAPPY BIRTHDAY plates and MAZEL TOV napkins. The type of graduate student who stayed in Londonville for the summer was the type to bring a plastic tray of store-sliced fruits and vegetables, some demoralizing combo of celery, carrots, and water-logged strawberries. Things untouchable. In this heat, Joyce supposed she couldn't expect much. Fine with her. Parties whose guests were well-fed were easily forgotten. Parties whose tenured professors lost control of their faculties—never. What mattered most to Joyce, and to everyone, was Simone's attendance. A department soiree was incomplete without the department's star, as evidenced by the potluck in June, when the biggest scandal had been her dog's escape.

People thought terriers were unintelligent, but Joyce knew her Humbert was sharp. The moment Joyce emerged ass-first from the closet, dragging a folded table on its side, Humbert commenced pacing and whining. Joyce considered asking Abigail to take him another night before remembering Abigail would of course be at the party. There was also the possibility of stashing Humbert in the upstairs bathroom for the evening. The upstairs bathroom was, in her opinion, the jewel of the house, with its clawfoot tub and window overlooking campus. The lock didn't work, but the room was otherwise faultless, and a small dog would be more than comfortable. But late in the evening, a line would form for the downstairs bath. Adventurous guests would make their ascent, flinging open doors and freeing captives. She decided to keep the dog in her bedroom and make a sign for the door. The sign ought to be clever, or humorous. She'd have to think on it.

As Joyce searched the house for Scotch tape, she paused to assess herself in the mirror by the door. She and Simone were the same age. Simone looked younger and was more striking, but—Joyce adjusted her tortoiseshell glasses—Joyce appeared more serious. No one would ever call her ugly, nor would anyone point to her author photo enlarged on a back cover, the faux-candid smile and coyly averted eyes, and scoff.

Joyce smoothed the front of her smock dress. She would not forget to call attention to the record player. Guests got a kick out of selecting records from her collection, which was tasteful. Women always chose *Rumors.* Men, *Closing Time.*

Ethan hadn't wanted to go out that night and neither had Simone. When they learned Ethan's novel had sold for fifty grand to a respectable imprint, they changed their minds. They felt happy. To attend a department party with a secret source of pleasure appealed to them both.

First they drove toward the highway to get Slurpees from 7-Eleven. Ethan was a simple man: he enjoyed the sight of his wife sucking up corn syrup through a big, green straw. Simone wore frayed shorts and a slutty top and had no intention of changing before the party.

"I have a theory," she said, passenger-side and slurping.

"Ouch. Brain freeze." They drove past Walmart, Buffalo Wild Wings, and what remained of a dairy farm.

"I think we are magic."

A pang of misery for Ethan. "What powers do we possess?"

"We fuck good news into existence."

"Have we done it before?"

"Yes. We had sex the morning I got into Yale, remember? And also the night before I got the offer from Edwards."

"We have sex somewhat a lot," Ethan said. He wondered what the cover of his book would look like. He wondered if his agent could get author approval into the contract. Was it true advances were paid out in four or five installments these days? He would never forget signing the contract for *Muse* and receiving, in the metal mailbox affixed to the brick porch of the house in New Haven, a check for $106,250.00 (half of two fifty, minus his agent's commission). He had walked to the bank with the check pressed to his chest, lest it blow away in the wind or melt in the sun.

"Here's my pitch," Simone said. "You're a Hollywood exec and this is my pitch. A middle-aged couple who never achieved their dreams has sunk into sexless middle-class malaise. At the urging of their therapist they have sex for the first time in months, and the husband immediately receives word his book has sold—at auction! Or similar good news. High on the thrill of success, the couple has sex again. This time the wife wins ten grand in the lottery. Or similar. They realize they are manifesting good news by fucking. They fuck their way into wild amounts of wealth and success, *but then*."

Ethan wanted to weep. "They get rid of the brass lamp they bought at an antique shop in scene one?"

Simone nodded vigorously. "They ditch the magic lamp they didn't know was magic, despite the proprietor's ominous comments and old-timey cash register. Now, their lovemaking has the opposite effect. Gradually they are stripped of their many achievements. If they keep fucking, they will lose it all, *however*—"

Ethan swiped at his eyes.

"They've fallen back in love. They want to keep fucking. They love each other again. What will happen?"

Outside Joyce Lockhart's house, he parked beneath a diseased elm, any limb of which could fall and crush their Subaru Baja.

"Can they return to the antique shop for a second haunted trinket?"

"Ethan, no." Simone shook her head with near-genuine grief. "The shop is forever closed."

The two of them crossed the party's threshold hand in hand. They ducked their heads in marital conspiracy before they parted. Ethan made a beeline for the drinks table, Simone for me.

"Robbie." She gripped my arms too hard. "If I seem prematurely drunk it's because I'm delirious with pride. Ethan sold his book. Listen to my pitch for a star-studded romantic comedy, which may or may not be inspired by true events."

Simone rambled with abandon while I drank my beer. We were girls, gabbing. I was a straight woman's scratching post. A fantastical salt lick.

Behind us, Billy from workshop said "Don't take my word for it. I'm merely a homosexual with a microblog." The house smelled like dill and deodorant. "Dreams" by Fleetwood Mac had played twice.

"You want in?" Simone said. "You want to co-write the script? Or maybe we could get you a walk-on role. I know, I know, you're not an actress, but—"

I believed I was doing her a favor when I said, "Your husband's headed this way."

"Well, good." I had offended her. "I like him."

Ethan snaked an arm around her waist. "Mind if I borrow my wife?" He passed her a shot of gin in a paper cup printed with silver hearts. No sign he knew my name or significance. I regretted resenting the allusions to her sex life. Better to have watched her strut all night than to watch her walk away from me.

Had Ethan noticed Abigail fuming in the kitchen? She'd dressed up for him. Her floral jumper was vintage, or vintage-inspired. She looked pretty and rumpled, like a chair a cat would sleep on.

Ethan and Simone slipped into the hall that led upstairs. I'm not proud of how much I hated them. On paper, nothing between Simone and me had changed since Ethan's return. We were still reading Woolf and training for the marathon. Still exchanging emails in which I sounded very young to bait Simone into telling me how very young I sounded. But I missed her expensive bras hanging from the shower rod, the

trail of mugs and books and balled-up athletic socks leading me to the professor eating figs at her desk or drinking a
martini in the yard. I wanted to return to her moldy shower
and call her on her shit. We were not men power-tripping in
a locker room. We were women in varying amounts of love.
She'd punished me for it, and no longer was I allowed to luxuriate in the *maybe* of it all. Maybe her addiction was not to jogging but to the bounce of my ponytail, the sweat adhering to
my upper lip. Maybe her fourth or fifth cocktail would inspire
her to undress me. Maybe she would take years to make up
her mind that maybe she was bi. But Ethan had returned, and
Simone had answered these questions firmly for herself. She
was too cowardly to tell me no — and too selfish. She wanted
both to feel secure in her commitment to her tall husband and
to keep me around. I saw this clearly, or clearly enough. At
the same time, anything could happen. People betrayed each
other every day.

Abigail stood beside me. Her movements were unsteady. We
knew each other slightly; it was she who enforced ten cents per
page at the printer.

"Do you know if there's another bathroom? I'm a dork, I
keep missing my chance to pee."

I dipped my chin and spoke beer-ward. "There's another
upstairs. End of the hall."

Was it cruel of me to tell Abigail where the bathroom was?
The woman needed to pee. The story needed to move forward.

In the upstairs hallway, Ethan tapped the paper sign on which Joyce had written:

> *Let the doors be shut upon him, that he may play the*
> *fool no where but in's own house.*
> *(Please don't let the dog out!)*

"Bedroom's taken," Ethan said. He and Simone found the lovely upstairs bath. "You could put a desk in here and use it as an office," Simone said. She made a habit of declaring what could be used as an office. Ethan cornered her against the sink and kissed her. She hoisted herself onto the counter, making space for him between her knees.

"What are we doing?" she said.

"Each other."

"Again?"

With imbecilic recklessness, Ethan said, "Forever."

She stayed on the counter while he got rid of her shorts and thong. In the mirror he could see her ass flattened against the Pepto-pink tiles. He liked that. When his pants were off they moved to a mat on the floor. Ethan imagined a future faculty party years from now, the crowd reduced to old-timers around a patio table, someone feeling frisky and polling the group: *Craziest place you've done it?*

"Department chair's bathroom," Ethan would say, simultaneously flirting with his wife and the idea of group sex. Why not? What fun was fidelity without a touch of exhibitionism? Either Ethan had forgotten his indiscretion or he believed they would soon reach the statute of limitations on cheating. A mistake could be negated by time, lack of consequence. And by powerful regret. Yes! The engine of his love was only picking up steam. Simone threw her left leg in the air to allow for the crooked approach Ethan preferred. The door creaked open.

"No," Simone scolded reality. "I locked it."

"I'm sorry." Abigail squeezed her eyes shut and failed to vanish. "I'm sorry. Jesus." She retreated, and Ethan lunged across the room to slam the door. He panted, panicked, turned soft.

Simone was flat against the bath mat, abs atremble. How could she be laughing? "Sorry your friend saw us fucking." She gestured for Ethan to crawl back in her arms. That she didn't understand Ethan was in crisis was entirely his fault. To his credit, he couldn't finish, and to Simone's credit, her amusement became concern. "Is it because she's a little in love with you? You're worried she's—what? Jealous?"

Ethan lay with his face in Simone's belly. "I'm embarrassed" was all he would say.

He failed to realize the incident had sent the exact message that most needed sending. Ethan and his wife gratuitously hooking up at a party for no reason other than lust answered every question keeping Abigail up at night. But Ethan was greedy. He wanted confirmation that nothing had changed—rather that everything had changed, but Abigail was not traumatized or unduly heartbroken by what she'd witnessed and would not be seeking revenge at this time.

On the stairs, Ethan let go of his wife's hand. He surveyed the party but didn't see his secretary. She had fled.

He asked Simone to get him another drink. "I need some air. I feel a little heady."

Simone nodded. Ethan often felt heady after sex.

Where was I? I was crammed into the kitchen with my dreary cohort. I was listening to Connie from Berkeley describe the nudist camp where she'd celebrated her thirteenth birthday.

"That's so fucked up," flash-fiction Larry said.

"It was a family vacation. We went every summer, but this was the first year I was mortified by all these decrepit, wrinkled bodies. One woman wore her pubic hair in a long braid."

Larry seemed to cycle, mentally, through several reactions before deciding the most Ivy League response was "Lovely." Past the two of them, I could see Simone pouring drinks for herself and her treacherous husband.

She knew I was watching her.

On Joyce's front porch, Ethan sank to a step and used his phone to write an email. He rarely wrote emails on his phone. He clung to a belief that the internet was a net negative for humanity, plus he didn't know you could delete the self-promotion the phone added to the end. I'm sorry you saw what you saw. I won't let it happen again. Sent from my iPhone.

Ethan returned to the party, sat on a couch between Simone and Joyce, and lightly participated in a conversation inspired by the sign on Joyce's bedroom door. Charlotte believed Hamlet was the original asexual. Two grad students agreed, and one was inscrutably upset. "Do you identify as ace?" Charlotte asked the unraveling one. Ethan mostly enjoyed this conversation, mostly enjoyed Simone's hand on his thigh. Periodically he remembered his book deal and hummed with private satisfaction. He had no understanding of the book deal as a consolation prize. A character who wants two things can have one, not both. Charlotte asked the student when they first felt no desire, and Ethan told himself the situation with Abigail hadn't worsened, not categorically. The future would be full of moments inducing regret and discomfort. What could he do about it now? It was no wonder Abigail had fled the party in despair. Fleeing in despair was a fact of life.

Ethan suffered from delusions of control. He believed he was a harsh, discerning critic of reality. Of what he was able to convince himself appeared to others as plain truth. And he was increasingly convinced there was no need to tell Simone he'd slept with Abigail. That Abigail understood and respected his choice. She wouldn't do anything irrational or unexpected.

It was a masculine delusion, traditionally, but Simone suffered from the same overconfidence. If I'm being honest, she was worse.

* * *

Abigail retaliated in the morning. She replied to Ethan's email and copied Simone.

> Hi Simone,
>
> He wrote this to me because we had an affair. I guess I was naive. Based on certain of Ethan's comments I assumed you were having problems in your marriage, but last night your marriage didn't seem too problematic.
>
> The affair is over now.
>
> Best,
>
> Abigail

Ethan saw the email while Simone and I were on a run. There was nothing he wanted more than to find Simone before she checked her phone. He would have given anything—including his new book deal and including his original book deal—to find her first. He got in their car and drove toward the lake. He pulled up to the trailhead the moment his wife and her student emerged from the woods. Simone's sports bra was soaked through with sweat, and the hair at her temples had curled and frizzed. Ethan startled her by climbing from the Subaru and shouting her name. He understood he was ruining her best summer. She had never been so satisfied with her work, or with him, or with the trajectory of their joined lives.

The moment their bodies made contact, Ethan sobbed. I had never seen a grown man sob and could have watched him all afternoon. Ethan seemed to savor the moment his wife believed him the victim of world-shattering bad news. The moment was brief.

"I had sex with Abigail. Just once. I love you and want nothing to do with her."

Simone let go of her husband's shoulders. The sunlight was harsh, revealing the dimpled backs of her thighs.

"Fuck, Ethan. I told you not to do that."

CHAPTER FIVE

Something to know about Simone is that, at age forty, she'd had sex with only one man.

Her first opportunity to lose her virginity had arrived toward the end of middle school, when she was prone to loitering outside the deli, making a turkey and pickle sandwich last all afternoon. Should she loiter long enough, the deli owner's son would eventually take his break and join her on the wooden bench. He had an associate's degree and liked to encircle her wrist with his thumb and forefinger, demonstrating how thin she was. On the first warm day of spring, when Simone was finally fourteen, no longer so ludicrously young, the boy pitched himself forward and performed the same test on both her ankles. She enjoyed this.

With frequency, and in the privacy of her bedroom decorated like a Parisian hotel suite, Simone conjured the boy's hands else-where — on her waist, crawling up her thigh — but her imagination lost steam when forced to contend with the boy's own body. Where would Simone's hands be during all this? She was indifferent, even hostile, to what this vinegar-scented, soul-patched man-child had under his clothes. In high school she collected admirers and rejected them when they tried to convert their admiration to action. She kept them inventing reasons to touch her hair — scheming to graze a hip or breast or buttock — but she couldn't afford to learn what would happen if she rewarded their desire. She considered herself worthy of worship and a sure disappointment in bed.

How could she believe either of these things, let alone both? I never understood.

Simone graduated high school valedictorian and with each of her male friends believing she had slept with all of them but him. Simone's mother threw her a graduation party at the house. Thirty of Simone's best friends and their parents. Black tie. Odorless salmon pinwheels on silver trays. Blossom Dearie singing "They Say It's Spring." After four martinis, Simone's mother — who would eventually sue the previous owners of the house for not disclosing the basement's elevated levels of radon, which may or may not have contributed to the lung cancer she didn't yet know was killing her — embraced Simone and whispered, "I like you, but I see through you." It was soothing to imagine herself transparent to someone, but the first part made Simone's blood run cold. A person does not want to know if her mother likes her. (This detail is in the memoir. Fact-check me.) When Simone met Ethan, she was as pure as the driven snow. There was no doubt in her mind she would undress for him. She trusted him completely. Ethan was the first person to whom she would offer her nonfictional virginity.

Something else to know about Simone is six years ago, Byron's father put his hand up her shirt. It was the anniversary of her mother's death, and Simone, having just read a mean-spirited evisceration of *Motherless* in *n+1,* was crying uncontrollably in the gazebo overlooking the wetlands at the edge of campus. Victor, a literature PhD writing on Dostoevsky, was taking a smoke break. Surrounding the gazebo flashed a mass of fireflies. Victor offered the weeping woman a cigarette. Simone accepted.

"I just found out my girlfriend is pregnant," he said, demonstrating that life could be worse. "I was in the middle of telling her she has no ambition. I'm a prick."

Simone knew him, though they'd never met. He had grown up somewhere between Valhalla and Croton Falls. Grew up entering national poetry contests and attending Ivy League summer programs for high schoolers. Smoked his first cigarette at twelve, joint at fourteen, lost his virginity to a lifeguard at the town pool. Took the Harlem Line to hear Phish at MSG and use a fake ID at Symposium. Was desperate to sleep with a

Brearley girl but never managed it. Simone, given half a chance, would have driven him wild.

"I'm from Chappaqua," Simone offered.

"Mount Kisco."

"We were neighbors."

"Wish we'd known. Would have saved me a lot of train fare."

"Doubtful." Simone stepped closer to him. She allowed his hand to slide beneath the silk of her blouse, his fingers to push up against her underwire. Her actions were not reckless. Her knowledge of what she needed from this encounter was precise. Pulling away, she'd said, "Have a good one," meaning night or life or baby. In Simone's mind, this was the closest she'd ever come to cheating on Ethan.

Simone knew she was nothing without Ethan. She also knew another man would have been better for her by being harder on her. Ethan hadn't minded when, in grad school, she'd failed to win her department's prize for best dissertation. If her first job had taken them to northern Nebraska or southern South Dakota, he'd have been perfectly thrilled. When her memoir was nominated for a National Book Award and she lost to a woman who was half eaten by a bear and lived to have the tale ghostwritten, Ethan's pride was undiminished. "You're allowed to cry," he said any time she cried, and "You *should* feel murderous rage" any time she felt murderous rage. A man like Victor, she knew, would have respected her less the more she failed. Would have gone through life as if writing a strongly worded letter to the editor.

The death of her mother, who for twenty-five years was the editor of the *New York Times Book Review,* had robbed Simone of the steely careerism that was her birthright. She had needed Ethan's unpretentiousness and unconditional love. It wasn't lost on Simone that without her husband she wouldn't have survived her grief. Still, she'd trusted Ethan never to return her to full-bodied bereavement. Never to be the source of all her sobbing and rage. What the fuck, man?

They abandoned me at the trailhead. They drove back to the house and neglected to turn the lights on, even after the sun went down. She wanted to know his darkest sexual fantasy and how long he'd had it. She insisted he rate the difficulty level, on a scale from one to ten, of letting himself come inside another woman. Inferring from Abigail's email that Ethan had betrayed Simone verbally before he betrayed her physically, she made him repeat the slander with which he'd disarmed his concubine. "You idiot." She laughed. "You unholy piece of shit." In her caged-animal agitation, Simone slammed each window shut. The possibility of me, worried, knocking tentatively at the door and overhearing a single note of Simone's heartbreak made Simone want to die. She soon found she couldn't breathe the air inside her home. She threw each window open. At this point in marathon training, Simone's strength was immense, her movements violent. The old windows shrieked as shards of paint flew from their frames.

Ethan sat on the kitchen floor. He leaned against the cabinet with the handle digging into his spine. Like a fool, he answered his wife's questions honestly, believing only complete and total debasement could bring him closer to redemption.

Simone kept saying "I gave you clear instructions not to fuck her" until finally Ethan, in a spectacularly misguided moment of self-defense, told her, "But I already had."

Simone was still in her sports bra and running shorts. Neither had eaten or felt they could. Their stomachs were concrete, their chests hard and hollow. In the rapidly descending darkness Simone sank to the floor and took Ethan in her arms. He gasped, and shook, and she said with her body what she couldn't with words. She held him so tight. She rocked him and shushed him, buried kisses in his rust-colored hair.

"The more I love you, the more I hate myself," Ethan said.

Simone agreed.

One problem with Abigail was she was no metaphor, no abstract stand-in for eros gone wrong or for mimetic desire or for the relation of the self to language. This was not *Lolita*. She was their secretary. She controlled the photocopier. Come September, they would see her every day. This problem, in all of its realism, was the sort Simone would typically face head-on. Tonight, she didn't have the stamina. Fuck Abigail. She knew it was antifeminist to blame the other woman—but Jesus, what a bitch.

Simone extracted her body from Ethan's and left him on the floor. This felt good, like managing to brush your teeth when you have the flu. At last Simone shed her stale spandex and started the shower. She let the soapy water run between her legs and avoided touching herself. She was miserable. Ethan had made her miserable. Even if she stayed with him, could she ever sleep with him again? What a shame. Fucking her husband had been the best part.

She got out of the shower and combed her wet hair away from her face. In their room she expected to see Ethan waiting on the bed. He wasn't there. She pulled on sweatpants and a bleach-flecked hoodie. Braless, defenseless, she went to find her husband.

Ethan was still on the floor, knees supporting elbows supporting collapsed head. He tracked Simone with his eyes as she hoisted herself onto the counter above the dishwasher.

"If there are more lies, we're done."

"I've told you everything," Ethan said. "I've told you more than everything."

"All you had to do was not fuck her."

"I'm an idiot."

"I'm motherless!" Simone bellowed at the ceiling. "I have no home! You were my home!"

"I still am."

"It's hard to be in this house with you."

"I won't stop you from leaving."

She wrapped her arms around herself. She spoke ferociously. "Do you want me to leave?"

"I want to never take my eyes off you again."

She said, "Let's get in the car. Let's go somewhere else."

They had no children, no deadlines, nowhere to be until September. They were accountable only to each other.

They drove all night across the moonlit expanse of western New York. The sun rose over Cleveland and scorched I-90 as they reached Indiana. They spoke not of where they were going or why; they remained in motion. They held hands above the gearshift. They stopped for gas in Portage.

"Gotta pee," Simone said.

Her crotch was hot from riding shotgun with her legs crossed. Climbing from the car, she swiped a hand over her sweatpants. They were dry. Parked in front of the minimart's entrance was a blue BMW. In the passenger seat slumped a young woman, pedicured feet on the dashboard, thumb caressing her phone. *Robbie,* Simone thought, then blinked away the mirage. The time had come to excise Robbie from her thoughts, or to think of the child a regular amount, or to start thinking of me, age twenty-three, as a child.

The cashier ignored Simone heading for the bathroom FOR CUSTOMERS ONLY. A silver-stubbled man in peak physical fitness paid for a Slim Jim and tossed Simone a single glance. She found she was nearly unwilling to circumnavigate the puddle on the bathroom floor, or to clear the cracked toilet seat of long, half-soaked strips of toilet paper. Her bladder throbbed. Nearly unwilling was the human condition.

The mirror was warped and ruthless. The ponytail into which she'd raked her wet hair twenty-four sleepless hours ago had dried lumpy and lopsided. At forty, her face was unwrinkled but far from smooth; without makeup, it was possible to discern craters left by stress-blemishes she'd picked bloody in grad school. Were the scars a turnoff? When she got back in the car, would Ethan compare her fading looks to Abigail's Mountain West maternity and reconsider which romance to salvage?

She shook out her hair and splashed water on her face. Like all knockouts, Simone was ambivalent about her mass-market sex appeal. The problem with Simone's appearance was she could never claim indifference to it. She would never be certain the author photo enlarged on her memoir's back cover hadn't sold ninety thousand copies by itself. Beauty existing in the eye of the beholder gave the beholder all the power. Everyone agreed: her beauty was her prized possession.

Today, she experienced the absence of the male gaze as a loss. She was an addict in need of a hit of being hit on. She had always known this addiction was adjacent to infidelity, but so were a lot of cravings she could forgive in herself and others. Much of what seemed to outsiders like disregard for monogamy or flirtation with marital ruin was really a performance of loyalty to her spouse. Simone's appetite for temptation was bottomless. She lived to disappoint all she tempted. It may have been a reckless game, but she'd trusted Ethan to play by the rules.

Simone tucked one corner of her hoodie into the waistband of her sweatpants. Her cause seemed lost, but when she emerged from the filthy bathroom, the man with the Slim Jim was waiting for her.

"Edwards University?"

Simone laughed in distress.

"I saw the sticker on your car. My wife and I were there last week? Week before? Beautiful campus."

The dead-eyed young woman in the BMW had been Adele, and here was her father-aged husband chatting up Simone amid the Ding Dongs and antifreeze. Simone should have known. She always told her students wild coincidences were the lifeblood of narrative. Coincidences and car crashes.

"We met," she said.

"I know. I didn't want to embarrass you if you'd forgotten." Without the distraction of amorous Adele and her rogue right hand, Simone could register the husband's handsomeness.

"I'm embarrassed you recognized me," she said. "You've caught me in a strange moment of my life."

"Are you on a book tour too?"

The vapidity of their exchange was unbearable. "My husband had an affair."

He bit off the top of his Slim Jim. "Your husband's a mad-man."

"That's one interpretation."

"Rumor is everyone who comes within ten feet of you falls in love."

A musician had said this about a famous singer-songwriter in the seventies. The singer-songwriter had been a favorite of Simone's dead mother.

"Was it a student?" the man asked. "I've always thought, if I were a professor—"

Simone said, "I don't want to keep you."

He chewed and swallowed and shook his head. "I don't do this often, but I'm a licensed therapist. If you need to talk, and you seem like you might—" From his pocket he wrested a bloated wallet, and from the wallet a business card identifying him as Dr. Spencer Shane. "Forgiveness is a process. It's a decision, but also a process."

Simone accepted the card. She wouldn't call him. All that mattered was that she'd gone inside a gas station minimart in western Indiana looking bereft as shit and left with the phone number of the man married to the girl who had, a decade earlier, tried to seduce her husband.

Simone wondered if Ethan wished he'd slept with Adele when he had the chance. Or maybe he had! That she'd never truly known him, that their life together had been a twenty-year delusion, was a tempting theory. Indulgent in its simplicity. The meat, definitively rancid, could be tossed straight in the trash.

But Simone's knowledge of her husband was nearly total. It was the nearness that kept her in love—and now destitute. Outside, Ethan had moved the car from the pump to the parking space beside the BMW. His forehead rested against the steering wheel. He hadn't noticed Adele.

Simone got in the car. "I'm smarter than Abigail. And more beautiful."

"Statements of fact," Ethan said.

"Do you understand how easily I could cheat on you? I could've cheated on you inside the minimart."

"I deserve it."

"I hate that you turned me into *the wife*. The wounded party. I've never let anyone imagine for a moment that you aren't my first choice."

Ethan was silent.

"Why did you do this to us?" In her pocket, she rubbed Dr. Shane's business card raw.

Ethan remained silent, but she knew why. He had mistaken love for something that could be tenured. Years ago, he had forgotten he could lose her, and she'd failed to remind him. They had so enjoyed what they took to be their freedom.

I have wondered exactly when, in this odyssey, Simone decided she was through with me. By the time they reached Portage, I had sent between fifteen and twenty texts asking was she okay, was Ethan okay, was there anything, anything at all, I could do for them? I had my suspicions — remember, I was there the night Ethan and Abigail rescued Humbert; the joy on their faces was both sacred and profane — but I pretended to assume death in the family. I buried Lois with the sweetness of my concern. By offering to swing by with a lasagna, I killed off one or more of Ethan's oversize brothers. My commitment to the bit was an invitation to Simone: *Play along. Write me back.*

She didn't.

Now, I want to get this over with. Rip the Band-Aid off. I'll put it here: when driving no longer became possible, they stopped to sleep in a motel whose parking lot straddled the Illinois-Indiana border. Simone lay beside her two-timing husband and silently renounced me. To survive this chapter of her life, she needed to believe in her innocence.

Simone became unbeautiful. She stayed inside the gray folds of her unwashed sweatpants, which she wore with no underwear, and declined to interfere with two zits blooming on her chin. Her odor was mostly armpit with notes of crotch. Simone had never in her life aimed to repel or repulse; she now wanted to weaponize her imperfection, to make Ethan reckon with her ability to be plain gross. But why? To assert her beauty had all along been a favor to him? Not true! Simone's beauty was for everyone, meaning entirely for herself. Did she aim to demonstrate he'd caused her unprecedented amounts of harm? That was closer. Simone avoided Ethan's gaze as he turned the key in the ignition. Neither commented on the wooden sign propped up against the motel's ice machine: HOME IS WHERE YOUR PLANTED.

Simone wanted Ethan to worry he could lose her. Without actually leaving, she wanted to be already gone.

Their waitress in Iowa City didn't notice their lives were in ruins. In spite of Simone's efforts, she did not actually appear repulsive or untouchable. She resembled a regular woman. She hadn't eaten since running twenty miles with Robbie on Saturday. It was now Monday, and the feeling in her gut was not hunger, but violence, like someone had dishragged her internal organs. Ethan ordered her a breakfast plate with poached eggs, toast, home fries, sausage and bacon, and a side of pancakes.

In the booth behind theirs, a man said, "She was barely out of undergrad when she sold her first novel!"

Ethan's face twitched with scorn.

Simone reached across the table for his hands. She loved his hands, which were large and hairy. His hands had made her come more than any other part of any human.

"I think it would have been easier to discover you'd been living a double life." Simone looked forward to a time when she would go years without saying Abigail's name. "Abigail has worked in our department for what, a decade? That you randomly fucked her is almost less believable than you having loved her all along."

"I don't love her." For himself, Ethan had ordered pigs in a blanket.

"Byron could be your son. I could be the mistress. Perhaps every time we've stopped for gas you've called her from a pay phone and assured her life will be so beautiful."

"Are there still pay phones?"

"It's perfectly common. People mistake themselves for the hero all the time."

Ethan put down his fork. "Her attention overwhelmed me. I thought it had to mean something."

Simone forgiving Ethan would not have been brave or radical. Forgiveness was the norm in marriage. Women had always tolerated men falling easily for oddball girls. These were modern times, and Simone too could toy with transgression. She could seduce a colleague or bed an ex (if she hadn't been a child bride) and expect forgiveness. No one would stop Ethan and Simone from having it both ways — or all ways. There were terms for these arrangements. The terms were defined in the dictionary, celebrated in periodicals. And if Simone didn't like *polyamory,* an unsavory coupling of Greek and Latin, she could coin a new word, write an essay about her non-marriage marriage, and this too would be celebrated.

"You can call her. I won't stop you from calling her."

Ethan said slowly, "I blocked her number before I deleted it. Abigail and I will never talk on the phone again."

"You'll miss her," Simone said. "You liked her enough to have sex with her, so you must already miss her."

"Simone, my love."

"And her son? There was no attachment there?"

"If you think there are choices I haven't made, if you think I'm in the throes of ambivalence over here, you are very wrong." He had never called her *my love* before. It seemed a miracle he had found something new to call her.

I should mention Simone's work-in-progress, because Simone was no stranger to polyamory—in theory. Her new book was meant to be a sexy, meticulously researched account of nonmonogamy in the twenty-first century. She'd received three different grants to finish it and spent the money traveling the country the previous summer, interviewing an assortment of deviants. She visited throuples in Amity, Arkansas; orgy-hosting ranchers in Dyer, Nevada; swingers in Fort Lauderdale; and for five days a philosophy professor at the University of Chicago who lived with her ex-husband and the graduate student for whom she'd left him. The manuscript brought Simone pleasure, even joy. Transcribing the interviews was the most fun she'd ever had. But the project was an act of varnished narcissism. The book, of which she'd never write another word, was a sham. Its only purpose was to create tension between Simone the myth and Simone the real. She would never write herself into her scholarship.

Really, Simone didn't care that monogamy was biologically unnatural. She wasn't a scientist, had never been seduced by nature. She was interested in what was beautiful and good. Sex was good. Friendship was good. Having sex with your friends could be—she acknowledged, even now—fucking good. But she still wanted the marriage on which she and

Ethan embarked in their Wooster Square apartment (built-in bookshelves, bay window overlooking Academy Street). Not because monogamy was traditional, not because it was tidy and straightforward, but because her marriage was her most cherished project.

He annoyed her when he chewed ice cubes — otherwise, no. Ethan was uncommonly gentle and generous, led everyone to believe he liked them a little more than he did. To Ethan, she could spontaneously propose any topic — the history of garden gnomes, Taco Bell's rebrand, Proust — and he would focus on her questions with the intensity of someone who had a dog in the fight. His face was the kind that inspired thin women to call themselves fat just to watch his brow furrow in that flattering confusion. He was tall, he was gorgeous, he had never in his life looked in the mirror longer than it took to shave. They had learned years ago to respect each other. When she believed he was wrong, she asked herself, *What if he's right?* If Ethan turned out to be wrong after all, who gave a shit? People were wrong sometimes. People were lazy and selfish and dumb. People were capable of infinite iterations of adulthood while remaining, at their core, a single implacable child. She stayed curious about the child he was. He remained her best friend. She had no interest in sharing her best friend with the department secretary.

So what if mating for life was unrealistic? From the beginning, she and Ethan had been unrealistic. To this day they still had their love, their complementary careers, their twin absent fathers, their inexhaustible common interests, their transcendent sexual dexterity. Simone wanted unrealistic. She wanted the exact version of her life she had promised herself—and Ethan had fucked it up.

With an ice cube on his tongue, Ethan said, "May I voice a selfish, possibly insane thought?"

Simone nodded.

"That message Abigail sent to my work email—"

"The messages you exchanged."

"The messages we exchanged on our work emails, do you think I could be fired?"

"Abigail and you are equals. You're the same age. You're not her boss or her teacher. You don't have any special power or influence over her. The affair was consensual, I'll assume. If she had been a student—"

"No, of course. If you even look at a student the wrong way."

They fell silent. Did Simone remember all the ways she'd looked at me? Some had been wrong. (Some were right.) She was nervous Ethan would eventually want to know where they were going and why. She felt convinced, abruptly, it would be his first question upon returning to the car.

"Let's walk over to the bookstore," she said. "We should stretch our legs."

He nodded and rose from the table. She sensed it would be a long time before he challenged anything she said or proposed. Admittedly, this was a pleasant perk of having been betrayed.

Parked outside the famous Iowa City bookstore was a blue
BMW, but they didn't see it. They each pretended not to
notice the other looking for their own book. (Simone's was in
stock, Ethan's was not.) As Simone let her eyes run unseeingly
over the spines of a thousand paperbacks, her mind wandered
to their wedding in the living room, upstairs neighbor's dog
silenced with a juicy bone. Ethan and Simone had vowed, *I
am nothing without you.* Had they meant to summarize their
meager past, or to project their mutual sublimation into the
future? Because that was what had happened. Ethan and Simone had made each other from scratch. Neither was capable of
a thought or sentiment unfiltered through the other. They had
their urges. Urges that caused Simone to wear Daisy Dukes to
faculty parties and Ethan to fuck the first woman who noticed
he was sad. But the lovable parts of Ethan and Simone — I'm
referring now to their respective *personalities* — were but
intoxicating flavors of the same marital brew. Abigail may
have thought she was alone with Ethan in that bed, but Simone had been there too. Simone was everywhere Ethan was.
And Simone hadn't consented to the affair. She hadn't welcomed the exploration of Abigail's soft, rosy fingers. Was she
wrong to feel so violated?

Simone looked up from a table of discounted memoirs and
saw a poster of Adele cross-legged on a stool, laughing pro-
miscuously. The author would be reading from her new book,
Everything There and Nothing Here, in this very store the evening of August fifth, if Simone wasn't hallucinating.

Dr. Spencer Shane appeared at her side. "I'm beginning to suspect you and your husband are following my wife and myself." As if characters can help following one another around.

Simone stepped back. Where was Ethan?

"We stopped for lunch," she explained.

"And what's next?"

"I don't know."

"You're on a journey."

"Eventually I'll decide to leave him. Or I'll stay."

"Stay tonight." Dr. Spencer Shane—whose childhood had been unhappy—stooped his shoulders and cocked his head. Simone believed without doubt she was being propositioned. "It would mean the world to Adele," he said.

"You mean if Ethan came to the reading." August fifth was tonight.

"Ethan, sure. But it's you she idolizes."

Simone nodded slowly. All she had left was a willingness to let things happen.

The hotel by the interstate had recently been a warehouse or a cookie factory. Now it claimed to be an urban resort. A chic supper club. An uber-luxe crash pad that shared a parking lot with an orthopedic clinic and a Jimmy John's. As far as Simone could tell, she and Ethan were the only guests. Failed business plans made her melancholy, made her think of boys striving for their father's pride, and she resented the burden of secondhand disappointment.

The pool was inside the building's former garage. Paneled doors opened to a lawn scattered with yellow Adirondack chairs and plastic children's toys. Simone didn't have her swimsuit, but she had running gear, and Ethan had his Larry Bird shorts. Simone swam unhurried laps. Each of her muscles felt strong and engaged. She was an athlete. She hadn't always been, but she was one now. Simone aspired to meditate but always fell extremely short of thoughtlessness. As her body sliced through the water, she thought, *I can never have sex with Ethan again.* Why not? Because he'd cheated on her. People cheated all the time—but he had made her so, so sad. She had been sad before, but now she was sad and humiliated.

Humiliation! Her feet pushed off the wall. What a relief it was to finally name the emotion shadowing and distorting her grief. What did Simone believe about herself if not that she was untouchable? No one would dare challenge her, or take what was hers. And no one had. Ethan wasn't an article or job or even her personal property. Easily she understood she was not these things to him—that her desires and impulses didn't automatically render her disloyal to her spouse and frequently amounted to none of his business. She was just some woman. A free agent wandering the earth. Could she convince herself Ethan was just some man?

Simone kicked harder, keeping her eyes squeezed tight

against the chlorine. She had devoted her life to entanglement with his. Body and soul. She had been certain of what he would and would never do. If anyone was going to cheat, shouldn't it have been her? (A thought everyone would have, when they found out what Ethan had done.) That she had the upper hand was a belief with which, she could now admit, she had always reassured herself. She wanted her belief back.

Simone returned to the shallow end and stopped for air. Running and swimming were not the same. Running did not mean negotiating with water for oxygen. Ethan stood at the opposite side of the pool's edge, his long, hairy legs bent at the knees. Without seeing her, he closed his eyes, pinched his nose shut, and jumped. Simone watched as he surfaced and swam to the ladder and did it again. His trance was childlike. She thought he may have been trying to exorcise an experience from his body—or having fun.

The water swallowed him. His body was a foreign country. Simone had known Ethan all her adult life and could not discover him the way a man likes to be discovered.

Discover was one letter away from divorce.

For the first time in days, curiosity surged between her legs.

To her reading at the famous bookstore, Adele wore tight jeans, a black tank top, and her hair in a long braid down her back. There was no mistaking the author's influence as she sat cross-legged on a stool reading an excerpt from her book about several married couples vacationing together in a seaside Italian village, their sex lives stoked and torn asunder by the scheming of a Machiavellian bellhop. At four hundred and fifty pages, the novel allegedly signified the arrival of an operatic new talent. The prose was incantatory, the plot a masterclass in storytelling. "Exquisitely playful," said the *New York Times*. "Bruisingly intense," moaned *NPR*. "Frenetically omniscient," claimed Judy with the verified Amazon purchase. Elegantly holistic. Specifically lackadaisical. Sweetly offbeat. The excerpt was fine. Halfway through the reading of it, Ethan whispered in Simone's ear, "What are we doing here?"

Ethan was a prisoner in the audience. Likewise miserable, Simone longed to do something to develop the story of her marriage past this moment in time. One option was to take Ethan into the bookstore bathroom and go down on him among the posters advertising all their enemies who had passed through town on book tours. Ethan's affair hadn't robbed Simone of the freedom to fellate whomever she pleased, including her husband. This was something to keep in mind. *Do it,* she thought. *Act. Execute.* But I will not saddle her with the indignity of the bathroom blowjob. Adele finished reading and Ethan rushed outside, practically gasping for air, leaving Simone alone drinking merlot from a paper cup. Simone was still alone, still drinking, when Adele asked her for a tampon.

Beside the meager poetry section, she brought her lips close to Simone's ear. "You know how it is when you're on the road and lose track of your cycle. I'm lucky these jeans are dark. I bled all over the stool."

"Sorry," Simone said.

Adele thumbed Simone's shoulder in forgiveness and bounded off to ask a nose-ringed employee instead. Dr. Shane approached. Rather than a paper cup, he held on to a real glass.

"My wife would like you and your husband to join the two of us for dinner after the event."

Where had he found the glass? What motivated him? "We're so tired." Simone was still in the habit of speaking for Ethan.

"It would mean the world to her." Dr. Shane wielded the same language with which he'd lured them to the reading. "She's somewhat fixated on you. I think breaking bread together would go a long way toward her understanding you as a real person, warts and all. We could make real progress here."

"I think you've misunderstood. She wasn't my student, she was Ethan's."

Dr. Shane patted Simone between the shoulder blades. "She rarely mentions Ethan."

When Simone went outside to inform Ethan it was time to break bread with Adele and Dr. Shane, what she wanted, fervently, was for Ethan to refuse. Unfortunately he was a broken man consumed with guilt and unaware that Simone needed him to be otherwise. He looked up from the curb where he sat with his feet in the gutter and said, "Oh. Okay then."

Adele took a century to sign books and flirt with fans. By the time she and Dr. Shane joined Simone and Ethan on the sidewalk, nine thirty on a Monday, most everything in Iowa City was closed. They took themselves to a dive bar where busted guitars hung from the ceiling. Adele ordered a collection of deep-fried appetizers, her tone a celebration of transgression. All four ordered cocktails. A rum and coke for Simone, to underscore despair. Gin for Ethan, who drank gin. An ironic old-fashioned for Adele, and a vodka martini for Dr. Shane, who hitched up the sleeves of his purple gingham dress shirt before experimentally touching an onion ring to his lips.

Adele pointed a fry at Simone. "You've done *Fresh Air,* right?"

"Sure," Simone said.

"Did Terry send you the questions ahead of time?"

"I didn't ask her to."

"What about *GMA*?"

"*GMA*?"

"*Good Morning America,*" Ethan said somberly.

"I mean, I know they'll do my makeup," Adele said. "But should I show up totally barefaced?"

"I did," Ethan said.

Adele frowned. "You were on *Good Morning America*? I don't remember that."

"You were in diapers."

Dr. Shane bristled at the word *diapers,* as if accused of something.

Simone hated Ethan. She hated him for allowing the night to unfold as it unfolded now. She hated him for his benevolence, his fortitude, the way he lit up in the presence of any woman less attractive and measurably stupider than his wife, as if his true calling was to bolster the self-esteem of dumb sluts. She hated him for hurting her feelings—for being the only man alive who knew Simone *had* feelings and hurting them anyway. He deserved to be tarred and feathered, hemlocked like Socrates.

Simone rested her elbows on the table and leaned forward. Her posture transformed the bar into her office, Adele into her student. "When you propositioned my husband at your college graduation, what effect were you hoping to achieve?"

Adele closed one eye and sucked whiskey through a straw. "When I did what?"

"Your hand," Ethan said. "*My answer would be yes.*" He understood Simone aimed to punish him and was supportive.

Adele turned to her husband. "Does that sound like me?"

Dr. Shane cleared his throat. "There are two possibilities. You may have wanted nothing more than what occurred. You propositioned your professor to affirm your fantasy of him, central to which was his faithfulness."

"Ha," Simone said.

"Or you may have wanted to sleep with him." Dr. Shane shrugged.

Adele's toothy smile was a party trick. She said to Simone, "For what it's worth, I think I was cool with it either way. I just thought, no harm in being honest."

There was so much harm in being honest. Honesty had fueled wars and burned cities to the ground. If Simone were being honest, she wanted to forgive her foolish husband. She did not hate him. The truth was she liked him very much. She was not incapable of reconciling devotion and infidelity. Urges — as in the urge to fuck your secretary — did not always complement long-term goals, such as not breaking your wife's heart. In doing what he wants, a man often accomplishes what he doesn't. But Simone forgiving Ethan would assign them roles: forgiver and forgiven. Loyal wife and cheating husband. Simone would have to commit to her part, convince herself of it, and trust me to corroborate her story.

When Simone got up to use the bathroom, Dr. Shane followed her into the dark hallway with its black paint and blinking bulbs. Beside a mop dried to a crisp, he said, "We're heading up to Missoula, then Seattle."

"Both stunning," Simone said.

Alone, she shut herself inside the bathroom. The lock twisted without engaging. She understood Dr. Shane had offered sex. Not an affair, but a chance to victimize her husband as he'd victimized her. And she might have been tempted, had Dr. Shane reminded her, as Ethan did not, of boys with whom she'd grown up, in their brown leather shoes and their fathers' old shirts. But Dr. Shane was from Indiana or Nebraska, some state of quiet lunacy. And still Simone might have slept with him to even the score, if she'd been able to persuade herself the score was uneven.

Let's be real. It was me who haunted her. Frequently she thought of my attention when she wanted to fast-track an orgasm. Had I been the one to proposition her beside the fetid mop—had I been bold enough to say *Let me touch you*—each word would have seared the softest parts of her. I would have given everything—I am giving everything—to avoid reducing Simone to the bit part of loyal wife. And if I'd been with her in Iowa that night, Simone might have let me go where only men had gone before. I don't think either of us could have said for sure.

CHAPTER SIX

The night Simone and Ethan dined with Dr. Shane was the night I hooked up with an undergrad. Maggie had stuck around Londonville for the summer to work on a local farm and avoid a family situation in West Virginia. We met on an app, and then at a bar called Toady's. She was older than most undergrads because she'd fucked off to Deep Springs for two years, and none of her cattle-roping, horseshoeing credits had transferred. She talked about Deep Springs excessively, referring to *the valley* and *SB meetings* and *isolation breaches* (derogatory). All of it was inscrutable and faintly threatening. At Edwards she was defined less by her experiences and more by her desperation to be understood.

A lot of fuss has been made over Simone's beauty, but let me state on the record and against any possible objection from envious members of my grad school cohort that I am also easy on the eyes. I seduced Maggie easily. I poured her a glass of Yellowtail chardonnay and fed her guacamole. I went down on her atop the red futon that had, during my childhood, furnished my parents' sunroom in Massachusetts. To the left of Maggie's labia majora was a misshapen freckle I mentioned to her afterward. Maggie said, "It's a birthmark. You can't catch melanoma where the sun don't shine." I explained I didn't enjoy receiving oral sex, only giving. Cunnilingus was something I offered my partner from the get-go so no one would ever suspect me of trying to wiggle out of it. Maggie, who had a ring through her nose and blunt brown bangs, said, "You don't like it because it embarrasses you or because it doesn't feel good?"

"It's like I asked for a back massage and the masseuse used her tongue."

Digitally, with digits accustomed to harvesting root vegetables, Maggie proceeded to bring me to feverish orgasm. Feeling like I'd graduated and could pursue some kind of advanced sexual degree, I asked Maggie if she knew Simone.

Maggie was vaping in her underwear. I resisted seeing the staunchly heterosexual honors student she'd been at her Appalachian high school.

"Sure, I know her," Maggie said. "I took a weekend workshop with her. It was for non-lit majors. I was going through a poetry phase. Vignettes about insects."

At the risk of revealing Maggie to be a revenge fuck, I said, "I had kind of a thing with her. Am having."

Maggie narrowed her eyes and vaped at me. The way her stomach creased when she leaned forward was so pretty.

I said, "She's my advisor, or will be, when I submit my thesis in the spring. We started doing this independent study thing but never really stopped. We're training to run the Syracuse Marathon together, or we were, until—"

"Skip to the sex," Maggie said.

"We haven't had sex. But she says stuff to me. She said, 'Let's be physical together,' while we were on a run."

"Is it possible she meant running?"

"Her husband went out of town and I slept in her bed." I omitted our moment in the shower, which even I knew strained credulity.

"California king?"

"Queen."

Maggie closed one eye, analyzing. "I need more information. Has she made overtures? Gone out of her way to touch you? Is she keeping you a secret?"

I couldn't remember. My certainty of Simone's attraction to me was born of the slightest inflections, the most anodyne comments syrupy with implication. The times we'd come closest to consummating our passions were the same moments we'd been most inaccessible to each other. The whole affair—let's call a spade a spade—had felt far-fetched and farcical yet intimately real. I badly wanted to produce an unambiguous example of

Simone's lust, but I had nothing. Since finding out about Ethan and Abigail, Simone still hadn't spoken to me. I understood that she was on a journey that didn't concern me, or more precisely — knowledge that lit me from within — concerned me to a degree she found uncomfortable. Still, the abrupt lack of communication was insulting. Did she imagine she owed me nothing?

"I slept in her bed," I said again.

"Do they have a guest room?" Maggie asked.

"No," I admitted. "And their house is a mess. Every surface is piled with books and journals and mail they're never going to open. There's nowhere to sit down."

My disdain for Simone's squalor read, plainly, as the symptom of a big fat crush, and Maggie went easy on me. "What do I know? I'll share a bed with anyone. I love people and hate boundaries."

It hadn't occurred to me that Simone's ethos was similar — that her affection for me was not actually a nascent version of what she felt for her spouse of twenty years. I wish I could say it occurred to me then. Maggie wrinkled her nose and passed me the vape. I plotted my next text to Simone, knowing it would go unanswered.

Cross SLEEP WITH A COWGIRL off my bucket list.

CHAPTER SEVEN

The drive between Iowa City and Denver would take eleven hours. "Why Denver?" Ethan asked over continental breakfast.

"Adele and Dr. Shane are veering north."

Through a mouthful of mini muffin, Ethan said, "Say no more."

The plains of Nebraska were, that day in August, yellow and windless. The enormity of the sky above I-80 gave Simone the creeps. She and Ethan had adopted a practice of driving in silence, which punished them both. They were sick of their own thoughts and terrified of what the other's might be. They arrived in Denver late and on the heels of a thunderstorm. They checked into the La Quinta downtown, watched lightning flash above the city and over the Rockies. Ordering takeout, Ethan was euphoric when the woman on the phone asked if he wanted his burrito dry or wet. He hung up, dazed with pleasure. "No one has offered to wet my burrito in twenty years." To the lobby he went barefoot. He returned, plastic bags hanging from his knuckles, and arranged the burritos smothered in ranchero sauce, the aluminum trays of beans and rice, upon the desk. "Dig in, baby."

Simone registered his happiness. No matter his mistakes, the burritos in Denver remained wet, the Rockies tall and snowcapped.

"What do you remember about our wedding?" Simone asked.

Ethan had sauce at the corners of his mouth. "I mean— everything?"

"Tell me."

"Simone."

"This helps me."

He pushed his food away. He leaned back in his swivel chair and covered his eyes with his hands.

"The day we got married I paid twelve dollars for a haircut on State Street. I didn't tell the barber it was my wedding day. Was worried he'd toss me from the chair, direct me someplace more upscale—worse, track you down and stop you from marrying a goon with no money. The guy put gel in my hair and I washed it out at home, then shaved, nicked my chin. There ought to have been a way to avoid bleeding from the face the day we got married, but our lives then — I didn't know how to avoid any inconvenience. Maybe I never learned. My mom surprised us, first by showing up in Connecticut of all places and then by giving us her mother's ring. Your friends arrived, and they were all smirking at us like we were doing a bit. Ginger was supposed to take pictures on film. Turned out she wasn't as analog as she claimed; she forgot to load the camera. Smokey took pictures on a clunky digital thing with a noisy zoom lens, but he died two days later. We never saw any pictures. Not that I need them. Upstairs, the neighbor's dog ground his bone against the floor. 'Tunnel of Love' played through borrowed speakers. You looked — so pretty. Not 'objectively stunning.' Not 'Hollywood levels of gorgeous.' Just this pretty girl I had found, whom I knew I'd love forever. You understood grief, but I didn't understand shit. I wouldn't say we did it lightly, but we did it easily. Didn't it feel easy to you? There was not a doubt in my mind. I felt so faithful. I don't want to take it for granted anymore. I want to live my life like I'm scared of losing you."

In Simone and Ethan's generation it was still possible to throw a *subversive* wedding. To defy convention while willingly indoctrinating yourself into a conservative cult. Women my age don't say yes to the dress. We say "Fuck you" to the Supreme Court and eventually, if we're lucky, "Okay, fine" to jointly filed taxes. Do I hope to get married someday? I do. I digress.

They sat together in near darkness; the only light came from the hotel bathroom. The love Simone had for her careless husband, it was worse than she'd thought. His twelve-dollar haircut had looked so good to her.

Ethan asked, "Should we plan our route to Portland? We could stop in Grand Junction, or Moab. I've always wanted to see Arches."

"Why are we going to Portland?"

Ethan looked at her with something like patience. "I don't know, Simone. Why are we going to Portland?"

Simone's unfiltered opinion of the American West was that it was ludicrous. Only a direct descendant of Charles Manson would crave eight-thousand-foot canyons, active volcanoes, tarantulas, scorpions, alien-choked skies, bloodstained sand. In obituaries back east, people passed away. Out west, they *succumbed*. What was wrong with New York state? Simone posed the question to Ethan several times per year, prompting him to clutch his heart and appear wounded. "It's bad enough we live here," he'd say, meaning the Northeast, the country's most regular quadrant. "We don't have to pretend it's good."

In Moab, the sky was a saturated blue at noon. The ridges enclosing the town were an otherworldly red. A black beetle perished on the asphalt beneath Simone's cushioned lounge chair, where she lay poolside with Ethan's shirt flung over her eyes. Her abdomen was pleasantly scorched by the time she felt him press a bottle of sunscreen into her limp hand.

"Be careful," he said. "The UV index."

Ethan was her family and there was nothing she could do about it now. He alone knew the foods she could stomach when sick and which pairs of underwear she'd had the longest. Divorce appealed because she could still succeed at it, whereas at marriage she had already failed. But divorce would not transform Ethan into a person she could live without. Simone was an orphan. That was part of the problem. The other part was she'd woken up with Ethan nearly every day since she turned twenty-one and she didn't want to stop—even now, she wished he would scrape his chair closer to hers on the concrete, wished he would refuse to tolerate distance between them. She refused to give him permission.

The pool had been empty when Simone closed her eyes. Now, water splashed onto her feet. Simone removed the shirt from her face and saw a six-year-old girl in a turquoise bathing suit, dripping and appalled.

"I haven't had a snack yet," the girl said.

On the other side of the pool the parents were seemingly asleep. The mom wore a tankini with loose elastic. The dad's hands obscured the shape of his pale stomach. He was missing a finger.

"I'm sorry to hear that," Simone said.

"Watch me," the girl countered. She pinched her nose, cannonballed, and laboriously dog-paddled to the shallow end. She heaved herself from the pool, again splashing Simone's feet. "Did you watch?"

Ethan, waking, blinked in the sun. "I missed it," he admitted.

The girl sighed. She struggled to free an excess of bathing suit from her butt. "I'll go again."

As she repeated the performance, Simone said to Ethan, "She's hungry. I think we have a granola bar in the car."

"Must be a hundred and ten in the car. Would a five-year-old eat hot granola?"

"She looks six," Simone said.

Again, the girl heaved herself over the pool's terra-cotta lip. "I have to go to the bathroom."

Ethan and Simone stared at her.

"When I was five I peed in the pool, but I'm six now."

Simone said, "Should we wake your parents?"

"Those aren't my parents."

Simone was scared to argue or seek more information. If the girl had been abandoned at a budget motel in Moab, and Simone needed to install a booster seat in the back of the Baja and enroll her at Londonville Elementary for September, she could do all that. In a world without milk carton ads and Amber Alerts and true crime podcasts (pedophiles, prison), Simone might have welcomed the child into her life. Why not? *You have a daughter and she sleeps through the night* was preferable to *Your husband had an affair with the department secretary.*

Across the parking lot was a bathroom adjacent to the motel's laundry room. Simone had on sandals, and the girl, who was barefoot, accepted a piggyback ride after testing the asphalt with her big toe. She went into the bathroom alone. Simone listened with a combination of pride and anxiety as the girl urinated, flushed, washed her hands, cranked a brown paper towel from the ancient dispenser, and emerged with her swimsuit twisted over one shoulder.

Simone refrained from untwisting the strap. The two of them pushed through the wooden gate to the pool. This time, the creaking of the gate woke the slumbering parents.

"What in the hell?" said the mother. "What just happened?"

"Calm down," urged the nine-fingered father.

"She took Caroline somewhere! Caroline, where did she take you? Are you hurt?"

"Everything's okay," Ethan said, rising from his lounge chair. "This is my wife."

"I had to pee," Caroline sobbed.

"I didn't want her crossing the parking lot alone," Simone said.

"Have you seen the news? There are people hanging around places like this looking for girls like her!"

"I know there are," Simone said. "I'm a mother too."

The lie disarmed the woman instantly. She wrapped her daughter in a large towel featuring the sisters from *Frozen*.

"I wanted to let you rest," Simone lied again.

The woman waved her off. The father patted his daughter's back through the thin towel. "Good job not peeing in the pool."

"We'll go." Ethan gathered Simone's books and shorts and sunglasses in his long arms. "We're sorry for the disturbance."

Simone followed Ethan to their room. She felt sunbaked and obedient. She understood Ethan had known taking the girl to the bathroom was a bad idea but had suspended disbelief, trusting what he took to be Simone's womanly instincts. She understood he was mad at her now and mad at himself for feeling anger toward the woman on whom he'd cheated. Simone enjoyed her temporary immunity to his disapproval—the way a person enjoys morphine in the ICU. Would there come a day when Ethan, self-forgiven, would hold Simone accountable for the mistakes she made this summer? She hoped not. Ethan's kindness was a comfort. Maybe they were both bad and could go on being bad together.

The room contained two queen beds quilted in desert tones. Simone flopped into a position she sometimes referred to, sexually, as the starfish.

"Would you have fucked Abigail if we'd had children?"

Ethan toweled his hair thoughtfully. "I don't know." Simone sensed his patience fading. Soon he would, for the first time since Abigail's email, lash out at her. "You never wanted children."

"I did want them. And I also didn't."

"I never knew that." In the bathroom Ethan threw his wet shorts over the shower rod. He pulled on Simone's unwashed Yale sweats, which were too small for him. Simone closed her eyes against the sight of the shins she loved. Ethan said, "I always thought whatever parental urges we had were somewhat satisfied by our students."

Simone ignored that comment. "I wanted it both ways and I had to choose."

"Why did you choose so young? We haven't talked about this in twenty years."

Because her mother died, and when her mother died so did Simone's understanding of herself as Mother. She would be Daughter forever, feet on the dashboard, lollipop stashed in one cheek, waiting for the doors of the bank to swing open and spit out the correct mother: hers.

Would it have made any difference if Ethan had stood over her hospital bed and watched her labor? Would he have internalized what he owed Simone (everything), and would the memory of her sacrifices have stopped his eyes from landing on Abigail? In my opinion, no. Children are irrelevant. Simone could have had ten of Ethan's extra-long babies, and each would have driven him further from himself, ever more desperate to watch another woman's tongue form the syllables of his name. But I've been known to underestimate the allure of the cishet nuclear family. There are reasons men and women reproduce and mark the heights of their offspring on the pantry door. For all I know, one reason is happiness.

Simone said nothing. She was willing to let Ethan assume she'd fallen asleep.

"You were always good at making choices," he said, starfishing on the bed beside hers. This was the first of the motel rooms to have two beds. Would they sleep separately? That Simone had shared a bed with Ethan every night since discovering his betrayal struck her as unbelievable. Next to him, night after night, she'd thought, *Something is wrong.* Then, *Sometimes something is wrong* until sleep had taken her.

"I forgot to choose," Ethan said. "I thought the wanting—wanting you, and to be good to you—would be enough."

"Abigail chose," Simone said.

"And I was receptive. All my life I've been so willing to give people exactly what they want."

"You'd have been a good dad," she said.

Ethan cried. He felt no anger toward Simone. He would have kidnapped Caroline if Simone had asked him to. Probably there was nothing he wanted more than to raise Simone's daughter, birthed or stolen. Where was their daughter? What had they done?

Approaching Boise, they used an app to book an apartment advertised as clean and centrally located. They arrived to find what was, unmistakably, the home of a young woman who had minutes earlier decamped to a mountain-biking boyfriend's place across town. An IKEA drink cart held the cheapest brand of every kind of liquor. Above the couch hung a pixelated portrait of Albert Einstein. In the bathroom, accessible by a sliding barn door, was a shrine to a dead cat named Edith, ashes and all.

The apartment made them feel crazy. Ethan went for a run. He asked Simone to go with him and Simone said no, and in saying no realized she couldn't run a marathon with Robbie in September. She had not run in days. Remembering how they'd registered for the race together in Simone's office, then texted each other pictures of the bibs that arrived by mail—remembering the twin holes in their neon-colored shoes—made Simone queasy with shame. It was worse than if she'd planned a romantic beach vacation with her student. It was worse, somehow, than if they'd exchanged nudes. It was worse not in fact but in truth: the marathon was about sex.

According to her phone, the mountains visible from the balcony were either the Boise Mountains or the Sawtooths. Running along the Boise River, vistas in view, would make Ethan as happy as a wet burrito. In his pleasure and in his solitude, did he miss his mistress? Would he call her? She'd pick up and he could say, "Keeping my heart rate below 150 just got a lot harder." Simone believed in the possibility. What did she want more in this moment than to hear Robbie's voice? Specifically to hear Robbie express disbelief that a man would dare mistreat Simone. *Simone?* Simone!

Simone called Dr. Shane instead. This phase of her life demanded recklessness. Everything had to come to a head.

"Where are you?" she asked.

"Missoula," he said. She was not attracted to him.

"Do you have time for a pro bono?"

"Sure. Adele's running a workshop. I'm relaxing in the room."

"I've never been to therapy. Is it like confession?"

"It can be."

"My husband had an affair, meaning sex, and I think I had one too."

"An emotional affair?"

Simone heard herself saying *Let's be physical together.* "There was no sex."

"But you feel your relationship with this person amounts to infidelity?"

"How about I tell you everything I did, and you tell me if it was infidelity or not?"

There was a pause. "Go ahead," he said.

"She—"

"She!"

"A graduate student. She's in her mid-twenties. I want to make that clear."

"Understood."

"Early twenties."

"Not a problem."

"I gave her work more praise than it deserved."

"A professor's prerogative."

"I fished for compliments from her."

"That's human."

"I did it so her compliments would echo in my head when I was sad, or bored, or—"

Dr. Shane purred sympathetically.

"We ran together, and afterward I would lean back on the couch in such a way she had no choice but to consider my abs."

Dr. Shane considered Simone's abs.

"I made up reasons for us to spend time together. Independent studies. Training for a marathon. I let her use my home office for an entire week while Ethan was —"

"Out of town," Dr. Shane supplied.

"In bed with Abigail." Simone felt the futility of making her crimes match Ethan's, but she pushed through. She excelled at pushing herself.

"Robbie's face came to mind sometimes when I was with Ethan. Or, not her face, but her words. The idea of her. The force of her attention and what it indicated about who I might still be. Everyone knows there's an expiration date on being the kind of woman I am, but Robbie made me think the date was a long ways off. For the first time in my life, I supposed if Ethan ever left me, the silver lining would be pursuing this person. This young woman. My friendship with her was nothing compared to my marriage. I never believed it was. But also, there was something absolutely pleasurable in it."

Dr. Shane quoted a Van Morrison song. Simone ignored him.

"Pleasurable, but cheap," she went on. "I constructed a self with whom she'd have no choice but to fall in love. I'm capable of that, because I've known a thousand Robbies. I've been a thousand Robbies. Easily I became irresistible to her. And then I shut her out."

"I want to draw your attention to something." Dr. Shane was abruptly alert, confident. This was his moment. "There are notes of hostility in your voice."

Onto the adjacent balcony stepped an old woman in a

nightgown. The woman pointed skyward and asked Simone over the railing, "No sunset yet?"

Simone shook her head apologetically.

"Beneath your affection is fury," Dr. Shane said. "You must always watch out for the person you hate. It represents the strongest emotional allegiance. Think, for example, of how you hate your own mother."

Simone lifted the phone from her ear. She resisted tossing it overboard. She did not hate her mother. If she had fleetingly and as a child entertained thoughts of hatred while enduring a time-out on the stairs, she'd been wrong, dead wrong to hate the dead. That the living and the dead were interchangeable was something Simone understood. Simone didn't hate Robbie. She didn't hate Ethan. Certainly she couldn't hate Abigail, whose mistake had been sharing the desire that governed Simone's whole life. Of course Abigail wanted to have sex with Ethan! Who wouldn't?

"Where did you get your PhD?" Simone asked.

"Don't need one," Dr. Shane answered cheerfully. "I did an accelerated master's."

"How accelerated?"

"Accreditation in eleven months."

From the balcony, Simone watched Ethan round the corner below, triangle of sweat staining his T-shirt. Her heart beat fast. He was almost back. He was coming back to her.

"Give my best to Adele." Simone never spoke to Dr. Shane again.

* * *

In Portland, Simone tumbled from their thoroughly trashed car and fell into the arms of her mother-in-law. Startled, Lois dropped her garden hose and flooded the dahlias. Why did these two women adore each other? In the early days of Simone and Ethan's relationship, Lois had been surprised to observe that Simone wanted nothing from her. Her other daughters-in-law required Lois to host their bridal showers on her screened-in porch. Becky and Jen insisted she invest, emotionally, in their kitchen remodels and choose a fun, distinctive moniker (not Grandma) for when they made her a grandma. They blamed her for their husbands' shortcomings and suggested new methods of styling her frizzy curls. They enlisted her as an ally in the psychological warfare declared by their own mothers: *Can you just call her and tell her the baby doesn't need her ears pierced? Can you just forward her this article on Sensory Processing Disorder so she thinks it was your idea?* Meanwhile, Simone had given up on being mothered. As Ethan's sad-eyed, ambitious fiancée, she had treated Lois with distant respect, as she would the provost of a liberal arts college.

The first summer Simone and Ethan came to Oregon as newlyweds, insomnia sent Lois downstairs at two a.m. At the kitchen table sat Simone in a large T-shirt torn at the neck. Reading *Middlemarch* and eating stale shredded wheat, she smiled up at Lois and said, "Night owl?"

Imagine having spent eighty-six hours of your life in labor and not gaining a single daughter. Imagine boys: their sporting equipment, their closets stuffed with socks and wires, the sour alfalfa smell of them. And then imagine Simone in your kitchen.

"Cereal? We can do better than that." Lois made a coffee cake from scratch. Simone wished she'd been raised by a soft-armed woman who hadn't died young. They talked all night, and so enjoyed each other's company that they gradually forgot a mutual relative had brought them together. "Only my oldest son is circumcised," Lois remarked at dawn. "With the other two, I couldn't go through with it."

Now Lois said, "This is a lovely surprise." She spoke with a mildness that had, in her youth, indicated poise and self-control and these days could be mistaken for fading cognition. Her terraced front yard smelled of sage and lavender. If Simone lost her marriage, she would lose Lois too.

"We'll explain inside," Ethan said. Simone wasn't sure how he planned to do that.

The house was a mess. Shoes were piled on the floor by the stairs, paperbacks straddled armrests, dishes festered in the sink. Lois's marriage had ended the year all three boys attended the same elementary school. Ethan's father demoted himself to long-distance relative; by the time Ethan was at Vassar, to stranger. If any of her sons reminisced about how tidy and organized she'd been in marriage, Lois would say, "I live alone now." An excuse, a flex. An ethos.

Simone and Ethan lived as if they lived alone. He never thought of her, discarding his underwear on the floor behind the bathroom door. Pouring the last of the cream into her coffee,

Simone thought only of herself. They had taken that Rilke quote too far. Her marriage had been lousy with solitude. Simone understood: she should never have let Ethan out of her sight.

"I have to talk to you," she said, pulling her husband upstairs, assuring Lois they'd be right back. Lois sank to the couch with her hands on her thighs, unfazed by turbulence. In Ethan's childhood room, where he'd had sex with Simone more times than with anyone else, Simone said, "You have to tell your mom what you did."

"I can't." Ethan said it so automatically that Simone knew they'd already had this conversation in his head.

"I love your mom. I don't want her thinking any of this is my fault."

"Any of what?"

"Our ashen faces and our car full of garbage and our de-ranged behavior, Ethan. Then there's whatever comes next. I can't lose her."

"There are no circumstances under which you would."

"Divorce."

Ethan took a trophy, filthy with dust, from the bookshelf. The soccer player had been bronzed mid-kick. She knew he longed to speak at length about the disadvantages of divorce. In his mind flashed a PowerPoint presentation entitled *Why She Should Not Leave Me*. That Ethan suppressed this lecture — drafted and revised and perfected over three thousand miles — was a genuinely moving testament to his love.

He said, "If you divorce me, I'll tell my mother why. You

won't lose her. I won't take Lois from you. But right now, today, I can't tell her."

He returned the trophy to the shelf. He examined the grime coating his fingers.

"Okay," Simone said. She wasn't unreasonable. "Then I need you to drive me to Abigail's father's house."

What a fool Ethan was. Even I'd have known not to look behind door number two.

Ethan located Abigail's father's house easily—too easily, Simone thought, as they idled by the curb. How often had Ethan been here? Was his sense of direction, abysmal in Londonville, unfailing out west? The house was distinctive. The house was pink and guarded by bear statues. Simone imagined growing up in the house, coming home from school and her mother not hearing, peeling wet socks from the bottom of the washing machine. Or Simone as Mother drinking coffee on the porch, supervising sprinkler play. Simone extinguished these fantasies in favor of the department secretary pulling Ethan over the threshold, finger to her lips. Bedroom at the end of the hall. No lights. No clarity. Simone imagined her husband's voice dropping to a whisper, Ethan saying what a man says when he lays a woman down. Simone did this violence to herself, but really, Ethan had done it to her first.

"Tell me what happened," she said.

"I had sex with Abigail."

"Tell me exactly where you put your hands."

"Normal places."

"Tell me where she put her mouth."

Knuckles rapped on the windshield. A bald man with white eyebrows and a narrow blade of a face shouted, "Edwards University!"

Ethan lowered his window. The man repeated, "Edwards University! In New York? My daughter works there!"

Ethan had no words. Simone sighed and said, "Bumper sticker."

"Aha." Her husband's relief was audible. There was some logic to life. "We're faculty."

"What department?" the man asked.

Simone's inclination was to cut corners. "Creative writing. We know Abigail."

Invoking Abigail by name, Simone eliminated the possibility of coincidence. She braced herself for the man's confusion, suspicion, wariness, astonishment. But no: he smacked a self-deprecating hand against his forehead. "My bad! I didn't realize she invited folks over. Makes sense, though. Diane went ham on the chicken."

Simone enjoyed this exuberant little man. "Ham on the chicken," she confirmed.

"Huge sale at Costco," he said. "Come in through the front when you're ready. I'll let Abigail know you're here."

There was a cautious hitch in his step. He wore navy blue sweatpants, plastic sandals, and a T-shirt reaching nearly to his knees. The man disappeared inside the pink house and Ethan said, haunted, "But Abigail is in Londonville."

"Apparently not."

"Please, please, my love." His eyes were damp and beseeching. "Please let's not eat ham with Abigail and her family."

Simone's door was open; she had one foot in the grass. "Not ham. Chicken."

She wasn't trying to be punitive. To not know what he knew—about the appeal of Abigail, or the interior of this particular ranch house, what had happened inside it and why—caused her physical pain. This pain was surpassed only by that of not understanding why she felt so bereft at the thought of a man and woman in bed together. That the man was her husband and the woman was not Simone was an unsatisfying explanation. Simone's book (no longer in progress, personally pulped) contained a passage on the practical purposes of monogamy. Beyond the containment of disease and basic scheduling constraints, monogamy served as a test. If you could trust a person to keep it in his pants, you could trust him with your secrets, your bank account, your lust and labors, your parents' end-of-life care, your children's seatbelts, your diagnoses, your pride and shame. But why was monogamy the ultimate trust fall? The standard was prissy, puritanical. Simone, an intellectual, knew that sex was not love. Sex could be checkers. Sex was often golf.

If Simone meant to punish anyone, it was herself. For succumbing to the baseness of heartbreak. The time had come to learn what she could endure. In the interest of mastering discomfort, she walked into Abigail's father's kitchen like she owned the place and, dismissing cardiac distress, embraced Ethan's mistress.

Horse-wild fright entered Abigail's blue eyes. She looked to Ethan for an explanation. Handsomely he loomed behind Simone and offered none.

"This is happening?" Abigail said. Over Abigail's shoulder Simone could see into the living room where Byron watched YouTube on a tablet. Adult voices narrated conflict between Barbies.

"Thanks for having us," Simone said.

"You were in Londonville," Ethan managed.

"I had to come back," Abigail said, drowning in regret.

Her father returned from the garage with a six-pack of IPA. "Cancer scare," he said cheerfully.

Alarm animated Ethan's face. His alarm was fleeting, but Simone caught it.

"All good now," said Abigail's father. "Need some help getting up the stairs is all. Let's eat outside."

No names were exchanged. They followed him through the sliding door to the patio, where Diane (sun hat, smartwatch) lorded over a platter of barbecued chicken thighs. Beyond the patio the yard was expansive and unmaintained; grass grew nearly to the top of the trampoline. Taking their seats, Simone and Ethan were joined by Byron.

"Hello, Byron," Ethan said, twisting the knife.

Diane said, "I didn't know Abigail knew professors."

Ethan, already stress-eating, had sauce at the corners of his mouth. "We're a small department," he said.

"Everyone likes Abigail." It cost Simone nothing to lie.

"Everyone likes to blame their problems on me," Abigail said. That she had given up on Ethan was obvious—and that she, as a result, had so little at stake made Simone very nervous.

"Sometimes people confuse the person who solves their problem with the person who created it," Simone offered.

Abigail ate her chicken with a knife and fork, showing off.

"Oh that's good," said her dad. "Abigail's always been a problem solver. I've always said that."

"To a degree." Diane looked at Byron, who was eating different chicken. His was cold and shredded.

"Sorry I can't cure cancer!" Abigail trilled insanely.

"If I were you," Byron said, eyeing his grandfather, "I wouldn't get cancer. I'd eat healthy and brush my teeth and always tell the truth."

As her father laughed, Abigail caught Simone's eye and mouthed, "I'm sorry."

Distracted by Abigail's flushed prettiness, Simone was confused. Abigail was sorry? For fucking Ethan? No. She was sorry because Simone's mother had died of cancer. Which Abigail knew, because Simone had written a book about her grief, and Ethan had also written a book about Simone's grief, and Abigail had read both books.

Abigail's father said, "Abby has an Edwards degree. She's a smart girl."

Ethan nodded as Simone said, "I actually didn't realize that."

"You could have done so much more with it." Diane's plate was mostly salad. Her credentials were unknown.

"I've always said being a mother is the most important work," Abigail's dad claimed.

"Wrong," Byron said. "Firefighter. Or prison guard."

"I'm not embarrassed," Abigail said.

"You have nothing to be embarrassed about." Ethan spoke so earnestly Simone supposed it would be less painful to watch the two of them fuck on the patio table. Then again, the visual had a calming effect. Their middle-aged bodies grunting and heaving among the overly sauced chicken thighs, the sparse hairs on Ethan's ass catching the late summer sunlight. What would Simone feel more acutely than pity?

"Dad," Abigail said as her father slathered butter on his corncob. "Not too much, okay? I don't want your cholesterol getting worse."

"Please!" Diane protested. "The man just had surgery!"

Abigail hunched her neck over her plate. Her bangs fell forward and Ethan glared at Simone. Simone wished she could communicate all this was for herself, not him. She wished he already understood. Accounting for campus interviews and visiting lecturers and department parties, this was likely *not* the most uncomfortable they'd ever been at dinner. But an argument could certainly be made. The deeper she got into her IPA, the more Simone believed she could turn Abigail into a character. A shared experience. A mistress could be demystified was Simone's working theory.

"Done," Byron said, pushing away his plate with indecorous force.

Abigail said, "You can play in the yard now."

"Tablet," Byron countered.

"Enough of the tablet!" Diane's hysteria was unseemly. The woman needed to take a breath, read more poetry. "His brain is rotting!"

Was Abigail's life as unendurable as it seemed?

"I've got my eye on that trampoline," Ethan said astutely. "Shall we bounce?"

Byron remained stoic for a long, suspenseful moment before he nodded. Ethan and Byron joined hands. Abigail's father said "What an interesting man."

Abigail began to clear the table. Simone was compelled to help. Simone, chronically helpful, hated to be waited on by anyone besides Ethan and his mom. In the kitchen they wordlessly chose jobs: Simone scraped chicken bones and corncobs into the trash, passed each plate to Abigail at the sink. In the yard the trampoline groaned and shrieked. A mammalian calm protected Simone. It was how she felt delivering a lecture or accepting an award.

"This is getting full," Simone said of the trash. "Can I take it out?"

"Pickup was today. I need to bring the carts into the garage."

"I'll help," Simone said.

They stepped into the embrace of a dry heat, daylight fading. A perfect summer evening. With confidence Simone crossed the driveway ahead of Abigail. She reached the cart at the curb, threw open the lid, and released a feral scream. She dropped the trash and the bag split open.

"I'm sorry," Simone said. A helpless creature clawed at the cart's insides. "Someone's in there."

Nothing had ever mortified her more. At her feet were chicken bones and a carton leaking juice. It was bad, but maybe it wasn't Simone's fault. Maybe this was the natural consequence of Abigail sleeping with another woman's husband. Maybe Simone was the one thing she'd vowed never to become: a victim.

Abigail lifted the lid Simone had slammed shut and peered inside. "It's a baby raccoon," she said.

"Rabies," Simone feared.

"The babies don't have rabies. There's a park at the end of the block."

They left trash strewn across the driveway. The cart's wheels were loud against the pavement, but their captive stayed still.

"I know you think it was about sex," Abigail half shouted. "But it was more like we were really good friends? Or trying to be. There was a conversation we were always almost having. The sex was supposed to get us the rest of the way there."

Simone found this explanation pathetic. If two people

couldn't manage to consummate their friendship with ideas, insights, jokes, and revelations, they didn't deserve to have sex.

"He's *my* friend," Simone said. "He's my best fucking friend." They stopped at the pine-needled edge of a wooded park, which didn't strike Simone as a park so much as the wild.

"Help me lower this to the ground. I'm sorry I tried to steal your friend. It didn't work! Congrats."

The cart lay between them on its side. Abigail lifted the lid and nothing happened. She gave the cart a gentle shake, and the infant raccoon made a slow, dazed exit.

"Now we walk away," Abigail said. "We don't want him getting any ideas."

Simone trailed Abigail and her trash cart back to the house. Abigail's eye roll of an apology had clarified something crucial for Simone, which was that no one could steal her friend. Simone's friendship with Ethan was a force against which even she was powerless. To entertain thoughts of divorce was only to daydream about a revised friendship. Tension instead of tenderness. Longing instead of satisfaction. But they would never stop talking; they would never stop looking eyes-wide to each other's soul. They had no other interests, not really.

Before they went back inside, Abigail said, "The sex wasn't even very good." And then, "He's not very good at it."

Go ahead, sweetie. Try to hurt Simone, cut her down to size. Expose the artifice of her marriage for what it was: a scandalous shtick, a sexy performance piece. All along Ethan and Simone had been teenagers making out against a row of metal lockers, then riding the school bus to an empty suburban home in whose carpeted gloom they stayed chaste and afraid. No. Abigail had miscalculated. Simone was certain of nothing if not Ethan's sexual competence. That he had been bad at fucking Abigail was music to her ears. Their little experiment had failed; they may as well have not fucked at all.

Simone got Ethan off the trampoline. Leaving was quick. Leaving was the best part. In the car Ethan took Simone's face in his hands and kissed her. Had they kissed since before all this? Had they kissed ever in their lives?

"I swear to God, Simone, if our roles one day reverse themselves, I have your back. I know this sounds self-serving. But I also know what I did, and how it felt. I was there. And you would have to do so much worse for me to leave you. I am nothing without you."

Ethan looked at his wife, and she looked back. Now was her chance to tell him about me.

"Suppose we never had sex, but I nonetheless did everything within my considerable power to make a graduate student fall debilitatingly in love with me before I broke her heart, arguably interfering with her pursuit of a master's degree and certainly warranting an investigation if the student were ever to file a complaint (or expose me through alternative, more creative means). Suppose I never touched her, but I thought about her while you were inside me. Suppose I never imagined I'd turn forty and want so desperately to be seen. Suppose I never imagined turning forty. Instead I imagined myself infinitely complex and you religiously devoted to me—and what if, in realizing my mistake, I want you even more?"

No. I want to be honest in my depiction of what I think she said.

Simone squeezed her husband's hand. She chose guilt over more grief. His and hers. What I think she said is absolutely nothing.

They stayed in Oregon one week. They slept in Ethan's childhood bed, and Simone, not by nature snuggly, found she couldn't sleep without Ethan's heavy arm draped over her waist. In the mornings Simone woke early and had coffee with Lois. They discussed varicose veins and Jane Austen. Lois preferred *Sense and Sensibility* to *Pride and Prejudice.* Simone mentioned her own mother had felt the same way. Lois was the one person to whom Simone had always spoken freely about her dead mom. It was as if Lois and Simone's mother had been old friends or fond colleagues. Lois expressed admiration for everything Simone reported her mother having said or done, which led Simone to tailor these reports to what Lois admired most genuinely, until Lois and Simone's mother were canonically soulmates-in-law. In reality, they'd never met and wouldn't have liked each other.

Simone felt unsure she'd ever confide in anyone about Ethan's affair. The cost—those closest to her choosing a side, turning on either Ethan or her—overshadowed any reward she could anticipate. She longed for a friend who loved Ethan and Simone in equal measure, as a unit and apart, who could accept Simone's devastation as well as Ethan's right to err. In theory, Lois should have been a contender—but, fond as Lois was of her daughter-in-law, Ethan was her child. Simone was no one's child.

She wanted it both ways. She wanted it many ways. To point a public finger at Ethan and say, *This man betrayed me!* To draw him close and promise he would never have to live without her love. To go on presenting their marriage as ironclad. To earn extra credit for her suffering. To divorce him and be admired by hordes of men. To marry him again. To humiliate Abigail once and for all. *To call me on the telephone.*

Ethan would get up around ten and revise his novel per his new editor's notes. In the afternoons they took long, sweaty walks to the waterfront or Washington Park, where they read Shakespeare aloud in the grass. They lounged with their ankles entwined, or one's head on the other's abdomen. They wore T-shirts and shorts like kids at summer camp. Ethan stopped shaving, and Simone continued not wearing concealer. When Simone interrogated these wasted days, when she attempted ruthless self-analysis, ready to face her delusions, excise her fantasies, she came up empty. She wanted to be close to Ethan at all times. She often felt tired and needed to rest.

At the end of the week they went to the coast with Lois and Ethan's brothers and their wives and children. The house belonged to the family into which Jasper had married and was in Pacific City, a short walk to the big dune. The children summited and raced down the side of the dune until their limbs were jelly, then returned to the house, where their mothers begged them to watch television. Lois did puzzles. Simone and Ethan's routine remain unchanged until the evening Ethan's brothers made him feel small.

"We need more kindling," Brian said.

"More paper is what we need." Ethan's knees were in the sand.

Jasper smirked behind his beard. "Think so?"

"I know how to build a fire," Ethan said, sounding for all the world like a little boy, embarrassing Simone.

"Okay, Ivy League."

Ethan stood. He avoided eye contact with either brother and went inside, his posture defensive in its perfection. In another life Simone would've followed, snuck a bottle of wine into the room they were sharing, and listened to Ethan connect Jasper's disrespect across state lines and decades to formative moments of fraternal abuse. But that life was over, wasn't it? Was she supposed to go on protecting her spouse from every pinprick of hurt?

Jasper's wife, Becky, came up behind him and slipped her hands inside the pocket of his hoodie. "You so mean," Becky said in a baby voice best kept private. Simone squirmed. "You is a bad boy."

"Mommy asking for it," Jasper warned. "Mommy testing boundaries."

"Jesus fucking Christ." Brian drank beer from a can.

"Punish Mommy!" Becky screamed.

Jasper threw his wife over his shoulder and hopped across the sand to the ocean, one meaty, tattooed calf at a time. Brian did the same to Simone. She opened her mouth to protest, to curse out her brother-in-law with professorial precision, but only high-pitched peals of laughter came out. Simone laughed from her belly button, from deep within her pelvis. Brian would throw her into the never-warm Pacific, and there was fuck all she could do about it. The shock of the water was wonderful. No reason to fight her way to the surface, not yet. Head over heels. Heart over toes. Her worst fear presented itself to her with abrupt clarity: for the rest of her life, she would have to introduce Ethan as her husband who'd cheated on her. "How long have you been married?" folks would ask. "Twenty years before he had an affair," Simone would say, rounding up. And however many since.

Her marriage would be classified as imperfect. Flawed, like everyone else's. It wouldn't matter that it didn't feel flawed, that Simone was beginning to suspect she loved Ethan more than ever. His affair had forced them to look each other in the eye and ask, *Do you still want this?* The answer was yes. The answer was so much yes it scared her. Their marriage was a triumph, but who would believe them?

At Yale, Professor R. J. Winters, an eighty-four-year-old,

six-foot-tall Woolf scholar, had been Simone's thesis advisor. Famous for referring to her students by their surnames, for breathtaking hostility, and for walking a leashed Persian cat through the cemetery, Professor Winters had been supportive of Simone's dissertation on the origins of the memoir. The professor was generous with her time, meeting Simone weekly for tea at the Lizzie. What Professor Winters wasn't was friendly. Simone had known nothing about her advisor's home life except what was rumored, and her attempts to share with Professor Winters her own unseemly humanity met with tight-lipped displeasure. Allegedly, Simone revered her.

Now Simone imagined Professor Winters answering the door in tennis whites, irritation straining her features.

"Would you stay with your husband if he cheated on you?" Simone asked in a panic.

"I don't have husbands," Professor Winters said.

Whatever Simone decided over the next day, week, academic calendar—she wanted to be able to respect these choices the rest of her life.

"Let's say you did."

Professor Winters let her inside. The house was less ostentatious than Simone had expected. The furniture brown leather and functional, the art original and tastefully framed. On the kitchen counter tussled two white kittens. "Brothers," Professor Winters offered. Outside on St. Ronan Street, a cross-country runner gave himself shin splints.

"Consider the following," Professor Winters said, pouring

cups of coffee from a French press. Her age-spotted arms were improbably toned. "Does your husband want to remain in the marriage? Does he admire you to a degree you find satisfactory? Was the affair ethical? Is he no less thoughtful than you are? Is he attracted to you? Are you to him? Do you have a mutual understanding of your marital conflicts and how you might solve them? Is there anything to be gained from forgiveness other than the moral high ground?"

Simone said, "Putting aside all that, is it possible for a self-respecting woman to stay with a man who stuck his penis in someone else?"

"A self-respecting woman?" The elderly professor's lip curled with disdain. Simone wondered if she could retroactively fail her dissertation defense.

"A self-respecting woman does what she wants."

Simone came up for air, wet hair plastered to her neck. She expected to be facing the shore but was turned around, could see only a vast expanse of breakers. Professor Winters had been dead three years. They had never talked about sex, or marriage. Professor Winters was uninterested in mothering Simone, though Simone had wanted nothing more. At the time, Simone blamed herself for being an orphan. But now, a fast-aging professor herself, she understood all her students as orphans. The mismatched socks, the stained sweatshirts borrowed from their roommates, the musty odors their backpacks belched. Grad students, especially, were orphans.

Simone swam to the shore. Her brothers-in-law watched her

pull her wet shorts from her ass. She did so with dignity. She took off her tank top and tossed it, sopping, onto the flames of the fire her husband couldn't build. So what? She hadn't married Ethan for his rugged masculinity, no matter what he believed about himself.

Simone went inside. She climbed the stairs to their room. On the pillow beside Ethan's open mouth was a dark, damp circle. He was stress-napping. If Simone had never met him, she'd have gone on assuming the tender pity she felt toward other men was love. Historically, female pity has fueled long, fruitful unions. But Simone was fueled by something else. It was adoration. Who cared how her marriage appeared to others? A house on fire could still be home. She looked at Ethan slobbering on the sheets and thought, *I do.*

She roused him. She told him she was ready to drive back to Londonville.

"You're coming home with me?" Ethan's eyes were lottery-wide. Simone's hair dripped saltwater onto the sheets.

It was excruciatingly simple: Ethan had messed up. He had ceased to be the only person who would never hurt Simone, had become a person like everyone else. In this way, they would be less like lovers and more like friends. In this way, they would love each other more than before.

When you're young, you think you're having sex when really sex is having you. Desire for a coed from ENG 304 sweeps over you like weather. Furiously, you try to satisfy it. Sex is consequence, not action. Then with middle age comes tragedy, comes terror, comes some colossal error in judgement. Middle age is when you have sex for the first time. Sex is now action; the consequence is the rest of your life. To perpetuate your autobiography, you must fuck. From this determination comes the phrase *make love,* an abbreviation of *make a love story.*

Which isn't to say it wasn't hot. That night, Simone and Ethan had the best sex of their lives.

CHAPTER EIGHT

Maggie and I were on the red futon watching prestige television. The program had been adapted from a bestseller adapted from an Edwards University MFA thesis submitted several years ago. Simone's student, surely. What had Simone thought of the premise? An infertile white woman nannies for an affluent black family. Loses mind, steals baby. Family unravels and becomes monstrous. In Maggie's words, "Painstaking political correctness resulting in savage racism."

"How do you think this works?" My head was in her lap. Her hands were in my hair. "You get paid for the option and also per episode?"

Maggie said, "I think when your infant goes missing you ought to téléphoner à la police."

It was the Sunday night before Labor Day. School started Tuesday. Maggie enjoyed referring to our situationship as one of two in which I was embroiled. Tonight I wasn't really thinking of Simone—meaning chief among my thoughts was *I'm not really thinking of Simone.* I was thinking of book deals and executive producer credits. About the dark moles scattered across Maggie's pale rib cage. We'd spent the last gasps of summer developing our own language and routines. *Lil Eddies* meant ten-milligram THC-infused edibles. *DHP* stood for dry herb pen. *Green Machine* was her favorite bong. We had become competitive about Mario Kart.

There was a knock at the door.

"Santa Claus," Maggie said.

I leaped up from the futon. I turned off the TV, licked one finger, and smoothed both eyebrows. Standing in the hall, Simone was tan and different, less pretty, slightly feral, more beautiful. She looked past me into my meagerly furnished living room. "Hello, Maggie."

"Maggie was just leaving."

My would-be girlfriend pulled on her shirt, gathered her items, and never spoke to me again.

Simone and her husband had been back in Londonville fewer than twenty-four hours. Her intention was to annihilate our friendship. I use the word *friendship* imprecisely. I don't know the term for what we had; I only know if Ethan hadn't slept with Abigail, we'd have gone on having it.

I played dumber than dumb. It helped I was already stoned. "Tell me again why Ethan cheating on you means we need to *reconsider the boundaries of our student-teacher relationship.*"

She straddled a stool, the wobbly one. "You have feelings for me."

"Everyone has feelings for you. You like it that way."

"Teaching is my vocation, Robbie. I'm not saying it's not complicated, but —"

"We took things too far."

She mistook my guess for understanding. "For me, yes."

"For others, not far enough." My feeble little laugh.

"To be blunt, I have suffered. I'm ready to hold myself to a higher standard."

In workshop my first semester, Simone claimed she could tell who among her students had suffered and who had lived painlessly. "Something to consider before you submit your various *autofictions,*" she'd said.

"This summer you've suffered?"

Simone confirmed.

On the futon, I sat up straight. For the first time in my life, I felt certain I could transcend discomfort, could tolerate obscene amounts of awkwardness, could (and should) choose tension over relief. "What exactly did Ethan do?"

It was obvious she wanted to tell me everything, and I knew why. I was not her peer. Simone's contemporaries may have taken pleasure in the sinking status of her once-iconic marriage, but Simone's marriage was nothing to me. The monogamy she practiced with that oversize, droopy-lidded man was the most cringe-inducing thing about her. On winter weekends he wore a hooded sweatshirt under a leather jacket. The way he ordered a coffee, you knew his dad had never loved him.

"Just tell me," I said.

Simone came to the futon. She unburdened herself. She spoke for hours and closed her eyes so frequently and for such long periods of time she didn't notice when, early on, I freed my phone from between two pillows and began recording. Certain details would have stuck in my mind regardless. Simone challenging Adele over fried appetizers in Iowa City. Simone spilling trash on Abigail's father's driveway. Simone's brother-in-law tossing her over his shoulder and into the Pacific. In me she confided much more than she should have, and it still wasn't enough; she left space for my imagination to run wild and up against its limits. (For those limits, and only for those limits, I am sorry.) By way of conclusion she said, "I'm dropping out of the race. My hamstring is tight anyway."

She left my apartment that night with the fatigued satisfaction of someone who'd completed a grubby chore—maybe a professional would've done a better job, but it was over now. Water seeping through the cracks was a problem for another season. In September I ran the marathon alone. The rain was relentless, the med tents understaffed, the signage bewildering. I accidentally ran twenty-nine miles, and it took five hours.

Between miles eighteen and nineteen, I thought my adoration of Simone had been refined into smoldering contempt. The feeling didn't last. Something I believed about eros as recently as last semester is that its truest expression is to love someone you can never have. I'm talking Elinor Dashwood finding out about Lucy Steele, resigning herself to spinsterhood. I'm talking old-fashioned pining, Keats, bleating in agony at the edge of the moors. Being Simone's secret suited me. Having her in this way, I'd keep myself.

I wasn't in her workshop fall semester. I was in Ethan's. I avoided office hours and eye contact. Avoided revealing I'd ever been or was still in love with his wife. Kept my head down while we workshopped everyone's stories: the immigrant mothers, love triangles, men on long drives convinced they're being followed. "Consider cutting the first paragraph" was my line. "Your story starts *here*." All I could think, when I looked at Ethan stationed at the head of the table, his rust-colored hair thinning at the temples, was that the man had nothing to teach me. Zero, zilch. Ethan wanted nothing from me. And I did not, in that season of my life, believe a person could give without wanting.

We workshopped my piece on a warmish, stormy afternoon in late October. The rain revealed how rarely any of us did laundry. Our clothes were rank with nervous sweat and mildew from the campus Speed Queens. I'd submitted a story I hated about a third grader whose house burns down in the night. She misses a month of school, no one knows why. She returns with tales of a firefighter breaking through her window and plucking her from a hell of smoke, of the aunt's house in the country where she and her parents waited for an insurance payout. She lost everything except Pandy, whose black-and-white fur had to be fumigated. The girl's teacher, impatient to start class, says, "Your house didn't burn *down*. Let's not be dramatic." All of this had really happened, except not to me, which was why the story was narrated from the point of view of a jealous classmate.

Masha said, "What does the protagonist even want?"

Larry said, "This is like your other stories: all atmosphere, no point."

"I love the sentences," Connie lied. "We can all admit the sentences are fucking impactful."

Ethan raked his man-hand through his hair. He scratched a jowl. What excuse had Simone given him for dropping out of the marathon? How recently had they slept together? What had he ever done to deserve her love?

"This story isn't about its narrator," Ethan said. "It's about this poor child who nearly died of asphyxiation. The narrative distance isn't doing you any favors. The device reveals an author who's scared to tell a story. Scared of dramatic action, of conflict, of taking risks and looking stupid. But that's life, isn't it, folks? Life is your mom embarrassing you at freshman orientation. It's going on a date and spraying yourself in the face with a bidet. I want you to question your framework, Roberta. I want you to ask yourself *who* is telling this story and *why*. Narration is the backbone of fiction. Something to remember next time."

I took that personally.

CHAPTER NINE

At home for Christmas, my mother gave me an electric kettle. My dad and I hiked up a mountain in the cold, and he asked how much I had "in savings." During this time, there were things I could have done to make my return to campus easier, or less of a crisis. I could have switched advisors. I could have dropped Simone's fiction workshop from my spring schedule, set myself up for a final semester free of mind games and abasement. But hadn't I earned my spot in the country's sixth-best fully funded MFA program? Wasn't it my right to study under the department's most celebrated faculty member? Certainly Simone had been within *her* rights to tell Ethan my grubby backstory, and I wondered—tortured myself wondering—how she had characterized my charmless mother and with what humiliating details she'd rendered me hunched over a stranger's toilet struggling to operate the mail-order bidet. Oh, how the happy couple must have laughed!

Let them. I had my own story, and Simone's only option was to supervise the writing of it. She was in no position to turn me away. Fucking with my feelings was an abstraction. Difficult to prove, legally. To fuck with my education was to flirt with a Title IX.

On the workshop schedule, I was slated to go first. It brought me comfort to imagine Simone, who had blocked my number, agonizing over this decision. Appearing to play favorites was a bad look. But having aggressively favored me all last year, Simone couldn't reverse course. Besides, was it even ideal to go first? Who among us had fresh fiction to share so early in the term?

I highlighted everything up to "sex without saying 'I love you'" and pasted the text into a new document. I made Ethan short and Abigail Latina. I changed upstate New York to rural Ohio. Yale to Duke. Dead mother to father. Then I emailed my submission to Simone a week before class, as per the syllabus. "Please find attached the first thirty pages of my thesis." (This was five pages over the limit. I made an exception for myself.) "Thanks so much! Sincerely, Robbie." Implied: Sayonara to my story collection. Everyone knows those never sell. I fell asleep on a black cloud of hope. Why hadn't Mom shelled out for a kettle that knew how to shut itself off? I woke up to smoke and melted plastic. By noon, Simone had summoned me.

Approaching her office, I was slightly triggered by the sun through the stained glass, the smell of hot marble, and her name—her real name—affixed to the door at the top of the stairs. Still, I ensured my knock was spunky. I listened to Simone roll her chair across the room, remembering that in the past she'd referred to this as an "undignified method of transport." At some point between then and now, she had stopped trying to impress me.

"Sit." She pointed to a half-upholstered chair with an unobstructed view of her Yale diploma. I sat. She sucked in her cheeks and said, "The pages you sent me, you can't turn them in. This *thing* cannot be your thesis."

Dumb as this sounds, her reaction took me by surprise. Yes, I depicted her getting fingered by her husband. Sure, I imagined Ethan hardening at the sight of Abigail's crusty eyelashes. But I couldn't have stolen such unsavory content if Simone hadn't granted me access. She had bared her soul in response to the caliber of my work. I taught her as much as she taught me. There was a time when I believed this.

"What's wrong with it?" I asked.

She looked at me the way you look at no one, when what I wanted was for her to look at me like I was the next Joy Williams, or a femme Denis Johnson. "Putting aside the breathtaking invasion of my privacy, the self-indulgent voyeurism and sentimentality, there are actual things at stake here. Careers. A marriage."

Why did I keep letting this woman hurt me?

"Fiction is supposed to have stakes," I said. "You've always been very clear about that."

"Fictional stakes, yes. If the publication of your novel would necessitate you hiring a lawyer—I'd reconsider."

"Is that a threat?"

Simone made her face blank. Bovine yet intimidating.

I said, "All authors get material from their lives. I mean, your husband's first novel was entirely about you. Everyone knows that."

"That was his choice. No one forced that on him."

"Didn't he force it on you?"

"He asked my permission, actually. We talked about it at length."

Which was something Simone had said a lot the year before. She and Ethan were always talking *at length*. She wielded their communication against me, suspecting I'd rarely participated in serious conversation outside of a seminar, outside of our friendship. She wasn't wrong, but I'd never understood what was so desirable about her and Ethan's verbose codependency. Breaking each other's hearts and discussing it at length—good times!

"You're right," she said. "Authors write about their own lives. But students don't write about their advisors' lives."

"It's also my life."

"You're barely in this story." She only had the first three chapters.

"I'm planning to play a larger role later."

"Robbie, let me be clear. For reasons we both understand, I can't control what you turn in to workshop or submit as your thesis. But let me be clear: if you write this, I will not forgive you."

The repetition disarmed me. She was scrambling. *Sloppy* was among the worst charges Simone leveled at her students. Sloppy was Connie changing a character's name from Stan to Steve but messing up her find-and-replace so the story ended on the word "substevetial." Sloppy was Larry beginning seven consecutive paragraphs in the passive voice, or Masha making her protagonist set down the same bag over and over.

As always, Simone knew what I wanted: Her respect. Her attention. Her lust and affection. She was daring me to give it up in exchange for a *Publishers Marketplace* announcement. The "very nice" deal, the mysterious auction.

No one had promised me an auction. I was ambitious, not stupid.

"This is my best work," I said.

It wasn't a question, but Simone answered: "Yes."

Here is how I want to remember grad school: The room at the top of Ryland Hall was oppressively hot. Everyone shed the layers of down and wool that charmed in November but repulsed by

February. The radiators clanged and hissed while the professor, in a tight dress and tall boots, her mythopoeic hair braided, endeavored to crack a window someone had painted shut seventy years ago.

Outside, snow fell.

I wish I loved something more than forcing others to read what I've written, but no: my heart swelled as my peers interrogated me.

"Why would he do this? Either he loves his wife or he doesn't."

"Where does this story really start? The chick has worked in the creative writing department since she graduated; the dude has been at the university ten years; they're approximately the same age. You're telling me this man woke up one day and, out of the blue, decided to fuck his secretary?"

"Is this story doing anything we haven't seen before? Do we need another story about privileged white people having affairs?"

"The handwringing over infidelity feels almost quaint, given everything going on in the world. Was that intentional?"

"Why does the narrator keep insisting the wife is beautiful? The word contains no information. I can't see this character in my mind's eye, and I don't believe the author can either."

"Do these people not have telephones? He should have been texting her dick pics on page 4."

Simone's workshop was old-school; I wasn't allowed to answer these questions. I was only allowed to take notes and look troubled and/or smirk. In truth, I didn't care if they hated the story. It was enough to know they'd read it and reckoned with it. My own power was palpable.

Simone asked me to stay after class. Neither of us moved from our chairs. There was so much space between us.

Defensively, I said, "No one knows it's about you. I changed the details."

"You don't know what they know, Robbie. I wish I could make you understand it's not up to you — what people believe, or how they feel. You don't have as much control as you imagine."

"I thought we were on good terms. I mean, you're still my advisor, and you admitted this is my best work."

Simone's face reminded me of being babysat by someone else's mom. If I were her kid, she'd have lost her shit by now.

"Robbie, I need to know who's on your committee."

"It's not finalized yet."

"I need to know you're not planning to ask my husband to be on your committee."

Ethan, though stigmatized by virtue of not being a full professor, was the second-best writer on faculty at Edwards. And publicly, his star was on the rise. His forthcoming novel had made several most-anticipated lists and received an early blurb from the author of last year's bestselling *Everything There and Nothing Here.*

"Your husband is the exact kind of person I want on my committee," I said.

Simone pinched the bridge of her nose, a gesture inherited

from her mother. She faced the window and addressed the snow swirling toward the quad. "This is an exercise," she theorized. "It's personal. You hate me, but you're not seriously considering publishing this."

"How could you read what I wrote and think I hate you?"

"How could you write any of this and not?"

Until now, writing had been a project akin to assembling furniture. It was time-consuming. It could satisfy if done well. There were playlists and snacks. The result was something I could almost admire, a new thing on which to solicit compliments. But this particular story kept me company at traffic lights and in the shower and in the warm, frictionless haze between lucidity and sleep. It was no fun. It was a compulsion. Writing this book, I forgot to eat. I could no sooner write something else than I could fall in love with a stranger on command.

Last summer, Simone fell for me. She took it back, as people do. But I was unwilling to submit to a history in which the falling didn't take place.

She said, "Your work has interesting ideas. A lot of them are wrong."

More than ever, I wanted to bring Simone face-to-face with her own hubris. Out of vengeance, but also kindness. The woman I loved still believed herself indestructible.

"Which of my ideas strikes you as wrong?" Spine straight, turtleneck clean.

"The suggestion that what I did with you is the same as what my husband did with her."

Old people were prudes about sex: what Simone and I did was way worse. But of the crimes committed last summer, worst of all was Simone letting Ethan think he was the only crook. Her husband reading my thesis would be catastrophic. His reading it would irreparably alter the narrative with which they'd agreed to move forward. Simone needed me to promise Ethan would never see the manuscript, to swear I would deny any real-life parallels in every future interview. My job was to be the little freak fantasizing about her advisor crossing lines Simone would never, ever cross.

Her anxiety was a joy to me. She believed there would be interviews.

"I won't ask Ethan to be on my committee," I promised.

Simone exhaled. That she seemed suddenly fragile was off-putting, erotic.

"I'll ask Charlotte instead."

"It *is* her field," Simone said ruefully.

"No," I told her. "Don't ever think like that."

We stood. Simone waited for me at the door. She squeezed my arm before wrapping a scarf around her pale throat and leaving.

That is how I want to remember grad school.

I spent the rest of the winter writing. I wrote through the mornings, drinking pots of coffee on an empty stomach, stopping only to shit and run fast miles. While running I didn't write so much as fantasize about the result of writing: an agent's breathless promises, a *New Yorker* headline tossing me to the wolves. Got home and wrote and forgot to shower. Once showered, forgot to get dressed and wrote naked. Went to class feeling alien or felonious, bewildered that my peers believed I was of their world. "I enjoyed it," I said of their stories I hadn't read.

"Which parts?" asked our fearless professor.

"The legible parts."

Simone glared at me from across the table. She became a footnote on the Simone I'd invented. She was a ghost. A memory. Harmless to me now. Around seven or eight I would close my laptop and pour a drink and plant myself on the futon. Will relaxation. Television? Porn? Poetry? By nine I was buzzed and ready to go again. Sleep was a vehicle for dreams, tools of my trade. In dreams I still felt the passion and the indignation, all of it. I woke up wrecked like a new mother. Opening the laptop day after day, I realized it had happened: I was what I wanted to be when I grew up.

Which brings us to the end of spring semester, to snowmelt and singing waterfalls, emails about robe rentals and course evaluations, the start of whatever real life would entail. For my last-ever workshop, I submitted Chapter Seven. If there's one thing I learned in grad school, it's that everyone loves a road trip story.

I could have printed the pages myself. I could have simply emailed the submission to my peers and left them to their own devices, as we often did. Instead, I sent the document to Abigail on a Wednesday morning and told her I'd swing by the department in the afternoon to pick up the copies. Certainly it was the most convenient course of action. One could assume I didn't overthink it.

It was the first week of May, and I shoved my dirty hair into a hat my cousin knit for me two Easters ago. Sweat beaded promptly on my forehead. My left knee hadn't been the same since I ran twenty-nine miles in the rain. Simone's office door was chastely ajar as she counseled Connie, whose ADHD always flared up this time of year. Ethan's door was likewise cracked. Every male grad student appeared to be crammed into his office as if in some kind of pre- or postgame huddle. The boys loved Ethan, which is something I left out of my thesis. It was rumored he'd once told Billy no woman had ever written a truly comic novel. That's another thing I left out.

Abigail had no office. Her L-shaped desk was in the department's open center, oozing with potted plants and piles of paper. "I'm Robbie," I told her. "I don't know if you know that."

She bit down on her smile. Abigail really was pretty. When she had slept and the light hit just right? She could have been beautiful if there had been someone there to let her nap every minute of her life. Across her desk she slid ten collated copies of Chapter Seven. I reached for the pages. She held on to them.

"I'd like to read the whole thing," she said.

There was no reason to tell Ethan's mistress everything. There was even less reason to send her some two hundred pages of my own dirty speculation. If I loved Simone, would I have done this? Could I have shut up for good and still loved myself? Lately, I couldn't tell the difference between restraint and repression.

"I'll send it to you." Maybe a co-conspirator was all I needed to initiate the conclusion.

"Would you like to get a drink?"

My first thought was I wasn't old enough. "It's two p.m."

Abigail's expression didn't change. Her palms were flat against the desk. "Up to you."

What I wanted was to make the moment last until Simone exited her office, saw us together, and got nervous. But I could hear her talking to Connie. She had yet to shift into her closing remarks.

"I wouldn't mind," I said.

Abigail slid my workshop copies into a stained tote bag she slung over one shoulder. In her car, which she'd left at an aggressively sloppy angle in the faculty parking lot, I nestled my feet among brown paper napkins, collapsed Happy Meal boxes, a receipt from the animal hospital. She drove weirdly fast, with sass, proud to have a driver's license. She didn't seem to notice the Joan Baez album playing through the speakers. She didn't comment on the undeniable fact that we were driving in the wrong direction, away from any part of town where we could conceivably get a drink. What was the grown-up word for kidnapping?

Adjacent to fields of cows was a sprawling compound housing Londonville's elementary, middle, and high schools. I'd never known where the children of Londonville were educated and had never wondered. Blue metal doors ejected a steady stream of tots with large backpacks. As Abigail got out of the car, a teacher in a brown skirt and Western boots jogged across the schoolyard to confront her. The teacher was animated, gesticulating frantically as she detailed the day's drama. The child who must have been Byron wandered from the school, unconcerned, and attached himself to Abigail. She scooped him into her arms, surprising me. Given my limited upper body strength and powerful dislike of children, I doubted I could do the same.

My heart rate spiked as the teacher waved goodbye and Byron approached the car. He opened the door and, with a bone-deep sigh, buckled himself into his booster seat.

"He's very self-sufficient," I told Abigail.

"That seat is new. Easier than the old one."

"Who are you?" Byron asked.

Abigail ran interference. "This is Mommy's friend Robbie. She's a big kid who goes to Edwards."

Byron said, "*I'm* going to Edwards when I'm a big kid. That way I can keep living in our house."

"You'll need very good grades," I said.

"I can read one hundred and nine words, but I can't spell them all."

"What was the teacher's deal?" I asked Abigail.

"Ms. Stacy likes to give me a hard time. Byron is this year's BBK."

"Baby what?"

"Badly behaved kid. Every class has a designated trouble-maker, usually a little boy. It's not that Byron isn't ever naughty, but the BBK is a self-fulfilling prophecy. People play the roles made available to them."

"What did he do?"

From the back seat, Byron said, "Don't tattle."

Abigail turned up the volume on "Diamonds and Rust," putting the child into a prompt trance. "He knocked over a desk. Sorry—he *pushed* over a desk. It was a deliberate disruption and someone could have been hurt. I'll talk to him tonight."

"That sounds stressful."

"To tell you the truth, Robbie, I don't really give a fuck. I'm not a bad mom, but no one's perfect. And the relationship between a mother and her child is as private and idiosyncratic as a marriage."

The seat belt was too tight across my chest. *Abduction* was the grown-up word for kidnapping.

"What about you?" Abigail asked. "Were you a good kid?"

"I never got detention or anything. I never cheated on a test."

"Your parents must be proud."

Byron sang tunelessly, and I regretted my choices. All of them. Back in town, Abigail parallel parked on a leafy residential street not far from campus.

"Did you still want to get a drink?" I asked her.

"I have gin in my freezer. I'll make you a martini."

It would've been so easy to say I'd run out of time. I had workshop in the morning, I hadn't showered or read anyone's submission but my own. Instead, I followed Abigail up the stairs to her apartment, where we were accosted by dogs, allergens, air freshener. Byron snatched his tablet from the kitchen counter and shut himself into one of two transcendently messy bedrooms. I expected Abigail to shake her head, to make a point of explaining that my presence had caused a diversion from their wholesome, screen-free routine. She didn't.

"Sit on the couch," Abigail instructed me. "Snuggle a dog. College students are deprived, right? You go months without experiencing affection?"

"I'm a grad student," I said. "It's not really the same." But I did sit, and a dog did climb into my lap. Half his hairs were wiry and half were soft. He trembled and smelled like Fritos. Maybe I did adore him, maybe I was deprived.

Abigail appeared, handing me a martini in a greasy jam jar. She sat on the other end of the couch and rested her drink on a pile of coloring books occupying the center cushion. "That's Joyce's dog," she said. "I babysit him from time to time. You know Joyce?"

"I've been to the potlucks."

"She's the department chair. So in a scenario like the one in your book, she's the person to whom your characters would report any questionable relationships."

"Good to know." I sipped my martini. The beverage was so incongruous with our surroundings, I felt instantly weary. The chaos would never coalesce into something I'd be willing to call my life. "Thank you."

"Then the protocol is, the professor character would recuse herself from her student's committee. All these rules are in the faculty handbook. I can send you a copy if it would be helpful. A novel should be well researched, don't you think?"

I'd read the faculty handbook. One problem with the rules was that they assumed the student was an undergrad, meaning a true youth, a potential virgin. Say what you will about America's automatically granted extension on childhood, but I was no virgin. The other problem with the rules was that they dealt in generalities, whereas Simone, a real writer, dealt only in the most fascinating specifics. There were no candlelit dinners, no kisses, no caresses or sex. It didn't occur to the handbook to outlaw sexually charged long-distance running. The handbook warned faculty to "avoid hugs when possible." Had Simone ever hugged me? My mind went to her fingers pressing into the flesh of my arms. My mind went to her abdomen, which she flexed and relaxed at will. Personally, I had no idea how to flex my abs. I could sooner wiggle my ears.

"The thing is, the relationship in my book isn't supposed to be black-and-white. It's supposed to be ambiguous whether the professor really did anything wrong. The point is it's hard to define what constitutes romance. Or betrayal."

Abigail got too close to me. "Based on the excerpt I read, it's a clear case of a faculty member abusing her power."

My drink was half gone. "I don't want to get anyone fired."

"You understand you're the victim, don't you, Roberta?"

"I'm not interested in being that."

"Well, sweetie, Simone still has her career. Her perfect marriage. Meanwhile, you sacrificed a year of your education to her psychodrama and got your heart broken besides."

"I didn't sacrifice anything." Abigail had read my chapter without saying if she liked it. Did she hate it? Did she skim everything that wasn't about her? Was the book—this had genuinely never occurred to me—boring? "If I want anything, it's the right to my manuscript. I want this book to be a real book someday."

"You were in Ethan's workshop last semester. I made your copies. You didn't turn this in."

"No."

"So you're in one of the top MFA programs in the country, and you're hiding your best work from your professors. And you say you're not the victim?"

I thought of the decoy fiction I submitted to Ethan. That cloyingly juvenile story about the house fire. I knew I was the best writer in my cohort. I was the only one who knew.

"Who's on your committee?" Abigail reached for her empty glass, took a phantom sip.

I could tell when I was being manipulated. "Simone and Joyce and Charlotte."

"The trauma lady?"

"She prefers trauma *scholar*."

"Ethan should be on your committee. Now that he's sold his book, he has the second-best CV in the department."

Byron burst from his room, shrieking about his tablet's low

battery. "Calm down," Abigail advised him, holding my gaze. Byron flew off the handle. He was in the middle of a game; his mother should've remembered to charge the tablet overnight. She didn't love him. Her disposition toward her only son was hostile. She preferred her job. She preferred the dogs. He didn't love her either.

"I'm sorry to hear that," Abigail said.

I ejected Humbert from my lap. Abigail followed me to the door while Byron raged. From the oversize tote bag she'd plopped atop a mountain of sneakers (women's size ten, boys' size tiny), she produced my workshop copies. I had forgotten about them.

"Thank you for the cocktail," I said.

"Robbie." She pressed the papers into my hands. "Don't let her walk all over you."

What did Abigail want? Justice for single moms? To abolish the academy? I never got a good read on her; my best guess was she suffered from divine madness.

I made my eyes vacant and polite. Gone was my chance to ask to use the bathroom, and I badly needed to pee.

She said, "To whom do you owe loyalty? At your age? I mean, really."

Submitting Chapter Seven for workshop was not an intentional act of violence. It was a love letter. She was already at the head of the table and acting so normal. She teased Connie for owning but one pair of pants. She offered Larry a stick of gum, and when at first he declined, she said, "I implore you to take the gum, Larry." As the workshopee, my designated seat was opposite Simone. As I squeezed in, Simone removed the elastic from her hair, shook out her mane, and tied it anew. As in winter, the room was ten degrees too warm.

Around the long table etched with twentieth-century student couplings, each of my peers fingered a copy of my chapter. The pages were a mess of exclamation points, underlines, heart-eye emojis drawn in ballpoint ink. An anticipatory heat pooled in my pelvis. The feeling I got before workshop was sexual. What is sex, if not attention?

"Shall we dive in?" asked my professor.

"I loved it," Connie said, breaking Simone's number one rule: no declarations of love or loathing. "The characters felt so real this time. Fucked up, but real."

"And the conflict," Larry added, "it's genuinely complex and rendered as such. How do we separate our intellectual truths from our emotional truths? So monogamy is a social construct — so fucking what?"

I was feeling kind of hetero about Larry.

Billy said, "The manuscript is really taking shape. The scene where she goes underwater and has the whole epiphany via her dead thesis advisor — " Simone shifted in her seat. She watched Billy with maternal absorption, as if deeply invested in whether he was capable of making sense. "It's trippy, right? It's magical realism adjacent?"

For twenty minutes, I knew popularity. No one had ever won workshop the way I was winning workshop. Simone's remarks came at the end.

"What I most admire about the manuscript is the point of view. The occasional emergence of a first-person narrator lends the novel so much texture and, indeed, intimacy. It turns the novel, otherwise narrated from the close-third, into a meditation on perspective itself. Has the author exposed the myth of the neutral narrator?"

Take that, Ethan.

I made eye contact with Simone, and I saw her love for her spouse, her fraught relationship with her own beauty. Her motherlessness, astonishing strength, fear of wild animals. She was a perfectionist, anal to the ninth degree. And she was a slob, a romantic, a sex fiend. Nothing meant more to her than the legend of herself—except the rare person with whom she fell in love.

I saw her, and because of her, I could write it down. I could make it so pretty. If she regretted the particulars of our friendship, allow me to remind her of their source.

Simone said, "I will caution the author to avoid self-indulgence. The framework is clever, but cleverness is a condiment, not a meal. The narrative at the heart of this exercise needs to stand on its own. If I strip this novel of its conceits, do I still have a story?"

It is my earnest opinion that a good class is holier than God. I've never shared that thought with anyone.

"Would the author like to respond?" Simone asked.

As far as I knew, I was Simone's best student. What we had, we came by honestly and could have again. Simone didn't have to be a prisoner of Ethan's indiscretions; she needed only to let the pedestrian stupidity of her handsome husband set her free.

"Thanks for the feedback," I said. "I hope it's clear I love these characters. All of them. I hope they don't feel like caricatures or parodies of themselves."

"Super clear," Connie said.

I would miss grad school. I would miss not knowing what was going to happen to me.

Campus was in full bloom, lush with undergraduates throwing frisbees, tying hammocks to the trees. Birds sang, probably. I played Leonard Cohen through my headphones and ran hard, deaf to my own breathing, my feet striking the pavement. On mile three, approaching the lake, the contours of my desires became known to me.

Over the past academic year, I'd endeavored to see the situation clearly. I had tried to puzzle out who betrayed whom; who remained in love and who was merely greedy. I'd been over the numbers, calculating what Simone owed and was owed, if I was in her debt or she mine. None of this was easy. Easier choices were available to me—such as letting go, moving on. Was writing a book the path of most resistance?

I lied to Abigail. For months now I'd lied to myself. I would have sacrificed the manuscript if it meant getting everything else. Happily I'd have burned these pages and written a brand-new thesis in exchange for Ethan knowing his wife fell for me. In exchange for Simone admitting the same and taking me back. I'm no psychopath. No visions of white dresses danced in my head. I was sure she'd never rent a U-Haul in my name or impregnate me with purchased sperm. Qualifying for Boston together would have been fun. Or if we'd completed our close reading of *Mrs. Dalloway* and co-authored an article. As my first love and mentor, she ought to blurb my debut. Send me inappropriately wistful emails a few times per year. Was she not entitled to a single night of passion with her protégé? Ethan got to fuck his friend! All Simone and I ever did was invent new depths of wanting.

I finished a lap around the lake, the trail hardening after a soft spring. Back on the road into town, cars flew past my left shoulder, I didn't hear them until they'd overtaken me. My whole body flinched, short-circuited, kept running. Adrenaline was something to want in its own right. Sweat sliding down my neck and pooling between my tits was wantable. That everyone deserved all information available was something I'd come to believe. What happened between Simone and me was information I could make available. I had that power. A car hit me. I was airborne, then sprawled across the hot pavement. Hadn't I looked? Where was my attention?

The sky was such a saturated blue. How sad to never run

again, paralyzed at twenty-four. Ethan climbed from his Subaru Baja, the honey-hued leather of his shoes so handsomely worn.

"I'm so sorry," he said, looming over me, eclipsing the sun. "So profoundly sorry." He was youthful, one of those men who would get hotter and hotter until the day he shit his pants. "I apologize." Ethan was careful to avoid victim blaming. He had become a connoisseur of apologies. He was the man for this job. "I did not expect you to do what you did."

"I was in the zone."

The pain, which at the moment of impact electrified me, had localized. One hip would bruise. My elbow was bleeding and my palms were scraped, but I was okay. No need to call the bluff of my university-sponsored health insurance.

"Let's get you out of the road." Ethan helped me to my feet. My okayness descended on us like a holiday, something sunny and American to celebrate. With his hand on the sweat-soaked small of my back, he guided me to his car. I got in without objection. His hazards were on, and I imagined the grim sense of responsibility with which he'd punched the triangular button, the phrase *vehicular manslaughter* ringing in his head.

He said, "I was just heading to the department. Our secretary keeps bandages on hand. Might be the closest place to get you cleaned up? Unless you think you need the student health center."

"I'm sorry I stink."

"Not at all. My wife is a runner—well, you know Simone."

Having finally uttered her name, there was nothing left to

say, and we drove to campus in excruciating silence. Simone had told me once her longest-held sexual fantasy was to make many men laugh the moment her husband showed up at a party. I thought that was weird. Simone, in my experience, was not especially funny.

Ethan parked in his faculty spot outside the creative writing department. I followed him into the building and up the musty, marble steps. His body was a stranger to mine. Our bodies were awkward about moving through the same space. His body was really, ridiculously tall.

Abigail ignored us approaching her desk.

"Do we have a bandage for Miss Green?" Ethan asked. His tone was pleasant, his head charmingly askew.

Without looking up, Abigail said, "In the kitchen. Did you run over another student?"

"Not *over*."

She slid her chair away from her computer. The air conditioning chilled me to the bone.

"Are you kidding me, Ethan?" Abigail relished the chance to be annoyed, aggrieved, inconvenienced by her erstwhile man. (When will we get a male word for mistress?) Me she fixed with a look of exaggerated concern. "Are you okay, sweetie?"

"Other than bleeding," I said.

In the kitchenette, Abigail bent over to rummage through the chaotic contents of an overstuffed drawer: flea collar, bag of sunflower seeds, a retired professor's expired passport. "This is nuts of you," Abigail said to Ethan. "You better hope she's not litigious."

"I threw myself into traffic." I assumed responsibility for the crash. There would be no litigation, at least not in a court of law.

"You were in the zone," Ethan reminded me.

Abigail produced a bandage. Politely, Ethan dabbed at my elbow with a damp paper towel. Bits of asphalt fell from my flesh to the linoleum. Smoothing the bandage over my scrape, he said, "Thank God you're okay. The program can't afford to lose a writer of your stature."

Abigail passed me a mug of water. A sign on the fridge warned graduate students that nothing within was meant for our consumption. I asked Ethan to be on my committee. I told him I knew it was last minute, the switch would gravely offend the trauma scholar, but Charlotte didn't know my work like Ethan did. Ethan knew how to read me. It was his approval, his signature, I needed.

Abigail stood radiant with triumph in the kitchenette.

Ethan brought his praying hands together. "When's your defense?"

"Next week. I'm sorry."

"It's a collection, yes? I'll get to read a revision of your house-fire story?"

"It's a novel now."

"You wrote a novel on top of all those stories? My God. You're prolific, you're a reckless runner. Are you my wife?"

Abigail took my mug and refilled it. Outside, the sun went down. Our reflections in the dirty window were soft, abstract. Most vivid was the turquoise sports bra Simone had lent me nine months ago and which I now remembered I was wearing.

"I'd be honored to serve on your committee," Ethan said. "Email your thesis to Abigail tonight, and she'll print it for me first thing in the morning."

"I already have it," Abigail said.

"Of course! I'll bring a copy home with me tonight. And you?" He turned to me, hands still pressed beneath his chin. "May I offer you a ride?"

"No." I was half naked, hydrating. "I'll finish my run."

Ethan nodded. "Admirable."

"Look both ways," Abigail cautioned.

I backed out of the kitchen. I wouldn't turn around until I'd left their line of sight.

During this time, a period of ten days before my thesis defense, I felt mighty. During this time, I mostly wore crop tops. Prowling around campus, I winked at undergraduates loading their belongings into their parents' SUVs. Londonville emptied; there were now places to sit at Manic Mondays. Free parking spots on Main Street. My days were devoted to lying belly-down on the braided rug in my apartment, marking a marked-up copy of my manuscript, tweaking, trimming, perfecting a book I was certain would change my life. Scratch that. Be my life. There was no Robbie outside this text.

The temptation to send the continuously improved novel to my committee members was powerful, but I refrained. Better to let them forget Robbie the unwashed graduate student, the insecure stoner, and allow their minds to build me anew: Roberta Green, debut novelist. 5 Under 35. Emerging voice. Stunning new talent. And such particular talent! To strip the committee members naked, to tear their fragile personal lives asunder.

My evenings were reserved for Toady's, the dive bar at the edge of town, whose open mic nights and poetry slams were routinely interrupted by trains barreling past the patio, rattling the wooden fence. When I arrived each night I was greeted by prospective PhDs who hadn't left Londonville for the summer, or townies of whom I'd grown fond: the custodian who entrusted me to hold the leash of his low-content wolf dog while he used the bathroom, the barista who never stopped boasting about the time he hiked the Pacific Crest Trail. I was popular here. Pitchers of Coors Light appeared before me. Strangers slung their arms around my neck and fell hopelessly in love. (Maggie, if you're reading this: I saw you from across the patio and didn't dare approach. All of this will soon be yours.) Those strangers weren't sure why they burned for me. I knew why.

No one is hotter than a woman about to get what she wants. Consider me a girl on the eve of her soldier's homecoming: fighting off proposals, fielding kisses. At closing time I left alone. I stumbled up the hill toward home, saving myself for her. Consider my logic: Simone barely forgave her husband's infidelity. Forgiveness took everything she had. The two of them put a Band-Aid on a bullet hole. Who could blame me for ripping it off?

CHAPTER TEN

To my thesis defense I was allowed to invite guests. Traditionally these would include close friends from my cohort, maybe
my parents. Instead, I invited Abigail. I told her she could bring
Byron, though I suspected she shouldn't. "I want you there.
You're part of this now." All I meant was she deserved to see
how the whole thing ended.

The defense was held in a seminar room next door to (and
the mirror image of) the one we used for workshop. Beside the
lectern was a long, narrow table where my committee members
sat like judges on a reality show. Abigail, Byron, and I chose
from a jumble of desks. With his hair slicked back and his shirt
buttoned, Byron folded his hands in his lap. His being included

in a ritual of such consequence had shocked him into obedience. My feelings for him verged on pride.

"Let's get started." Simone was all warmth and enthusiasm. If we had run that marathon together in the fall, she would have smoked me. "To begin, we'd love to have you read for five to ten minutes. An excerpt of your choosing."

I made my way to the lectern. The copy in my hands was the one I'd obsessively edited these past ten days. The sentences I read aloud were perfect, shimmering gems. Lucid, limpid prose. The word *virtuosic* might have come to mind. I read the opening. Last year's department party at Joyce Lockhart's house. Temperate laughter. Someone's sandalwood perfume. "Lola" by the Kinks. Ethan and Abigail slipping into the night only to return with the prodigal pet. Of all my chapters, the first was the most unabashedly inspired by true events. I had changed names, but there was no mistaking the crust in Abigail's eyes or Joyce's many beaded necklaces or Ethan's loneliness.

My reading ended when Ethan arrived home to find the wife he hadn't yet betrayed asleep in her sweatpants.

"I'll stop there," I said.

I remained at the lectern. It disturbed me that Simone and Ethan had chosen to sit next to each other. Her right knee touched his left beneath the table. In the brief but terrifying silence, I worried I'd miscalculated. Then Ethan moved his knee.

"I don't think I can do this," he said with the temporary calm of a mercurial father.

"You can," Simone whispered, adjusting the deep V of her blouse. "Just like we talked about. We can do hard things."

She reached for his hand, and Ethan withdrew as if wounded. He stood so violently his chair fell backward, and Byron gasped at the clang and the clamor. "We all know what this is," Ethan said. "Your student has exposed us. She's airing our dirty laundry!"

Men's rage issues are to their evolutionary advantage, and Ethan's anger was sexually confusing to me until Simone pushed back her own chair and brought my lust home.

"It's a novel," she said. "It can't hurt you."

"It is a thinly veiled account of my wife punishing me for a moment of poor judgement while secretly and continuously cheating on me with a graduate student."

"Goodness." Joyce rummaged through her bag in search of the relevant paperwork: termination letters, Title IX complaints, insurance claims, customer satisfaction surveys—whatever the situation required, she was prepared.

"Mommy?" Byron tugged on Abigail's shirtsleeve. "If the teachers get divorced, will Ethan be my daddy?"

Abigail considered it. "No," she said neutrally, and her lips froze halfway to a qualification: *But I might fuck him one to two times more.*

"We can get through this," Simone said, eyes fixed on her beloved as her faith in truth and beauty waned, or maybe wandered off in want of a new mascot (me). "We talked about this, Ethan. We both made mistakes. Our marriage is stronger for it."

Abigail hooted.

"I thought that too, until—" Ethan gestured in my direction. I had on my high school graduation dress, the hem of which fell short of dignity, and I was gripping the lectern for dear life. "Honestly, hearing your mistress read aloud her revenge porn was a bit much for me."

Joyce cleared her throat. "I just want to remind folks to practice hermeneutic charity, when possible." Our heads swiveled toward the timid sound of her. "A child is present," Joyce clarified.

Ethan ignored her and addressed his wife. "If you want to stay married to me, you will not approve this thesis." For what must have been the first time in his forty-two years, Ethan's voice boomed as if from the pulpit or the fifth act of a play. He sounded suddenly British, and my heart did sink. Flunking out of grad school wasn't a risk I'd meant to take. "If you want to stay married to me," Ethan repeated, "tell your girlfriend here to burn her manuscript and transfer to another school. I'm begging you, Simone, let your letter of recommendation be the last favor you do Roberta Green."

"No," Simone said.

My joy was shame-flavored. My shame seasoned with so much joy.

Ethan blinked. "No?"

Simone's top was silk and see-through, her braid pristine. "To reject Robbie's thesis would be a betrayal of my deepest pedagogical convictions. Her book is a masterpiece, Ethan. It's better than anything you've ever written. If you can't see when a writer's artistic achievement is worth our marital discomfort, perhaps you're not the man for me."

Byron's mouth formed a perfect O. He was more precocious than I'd realized.

Deep in the weeds, forms-wise, Joyce looked up and said, "So what I'm hearing is the manuscript was *non*fictional, and that an *un*tenured faculty member carried on a *sex*ual relationship with a university employee, and meanwhile a full professor—his *wife*—had more of an emotional affair?"

"My wife is in love with her student!" Ethan argued.

"Be that as it may, when it comes to determining misconduct, love is a gray area, and if the professor has tenure..." Joyce trailed off with an administrative clacking of her tongue.

Outside, snow swirled, or maybe cherry blossoms given the season. No, I realized, the peripheral flashes of white were scraps of paper. Graduating seniors had shredded their notes from the semester into confetti they were tossing out the upper-story windows. It was a tradition. School was a fairy tale. To think I would run out of degrees to pursue—that the MFA itself was considered terminal—broke my heart.

"Let's be honest," Ethan said to Simone, packing up his pens and papers. "I never was worthy of you. If your mother hadn't died, she'd have objected to the marriage. You wouldn't have gone through with it." Ethan seized his briefcase and pointed a crooked finger at me. "Best of luck to you. I mean that." Before he stormed out of the seminar room, he cocked his head at his secretary as if to say, *I'll call you?*

Abigail shrugged coquettishly. What a tease!

"I'm perplexed," Joyce said as the door closed on Ethan. "Is he voting to approve the thesis, or...?"

"Yes," the rest of us answered in unison. With the merging of our voices, Simone turned, at last, to face me. She was beautiful. From this day forward, she would prevent my worst behavior. She would save me from myself. "I'm sorry I made you feel none of this was real. I'm sorry I tried to convince you our love was in your head. In truth, I'm in awe of you as a woman and as a writer. You have bewitched me, Robbie, body and soul."

And with that, my advisor got down on one knee.

CHAPTER ELEVEN

Just kidding.

To my thesis defense I was allowed to invite guests, yes. And traditionally these would include close friends from my cohort, maybe my parents. And instead I invited Abigail. I told her she could bring Byron, though I suspected she shouldn't. "I want you there. You're part of this now." All I meant was she deserved to see how the whole thing ended.

The defense was held in the seminar room next door to the one we used for workshop. Beside the lectern was a long, narrow table where my committee members sat like judges on a reality show. Abigail, Byron, and I chose from a jumble of desks. Byron was attached to headphones attached to his tablet, and still Joyce cleared her throat and said into the awkward pre-show silence, "Is there any way our young friend could wait in the hall?"

Did the department chair find it odd that the department secretary had been invited to Roberta Green's thesis defense? She found it very odd. Abigail's uncertainty verged on panic. She lifted the headphones from her son. "Do you think you could play your barbershop game in the hall? Can you be so, so good? Mommy's big, brave man?"

Solemnly, Byron nodded. As Abigail shepherded her lamb out the door, Joyce leaned across Ethan's lap and asked Simone, "How old is he?"

"Almost six," Ethan answered.

"Perfect," Joyce said, a bartender satisfied by a glance at a customer's ID.

"Let's get started." Simone was all warmth and enthusiasm. If we had run that marathon together in the fall, she would have smoked me. "To begin, we'd love to have you read for five to ten minutes. An excerpt of your choosing."

I made my way to the lectern. The copy in my hands was the one I'd obsessively edited these past ten days. The sentences I read aloud were perfect, shimmering gems. Lucid, limpid prose. The word *virtuosic* might have come to mind. I read the opening. Last year's department party at Joyce Lockhart's house. Temperate laughter. Someone's sandalwood perfume. "Lola" by the Kinks. Ethan and Abigail slipping into the night only to return with the prodigal pet. Of all my chapters, the first was the most unabashedly inspired by true events. I had changed names, but there was no mistaking the crust in Abigail's eyes or Joyce's many beaded necklaces or Ethan's loneliness. I read without looking up to see them fidget, squirm, roll their eyes. Easily I could picture Simone slicing a hand across her neck, her favorite gesture, meaning *Stop talking* and *Kindly slit my throat.* I lifted my gaze only once to assess Abigail's mental health. She had stacked her hands over her heart. Her eyes shone with tearful pride, or recognition. I missed my mother, who, if she had known what I'd done, wouldn't have thought twice about shaking me upside down until the stupid fell out.

My reading ended when Ethan arrived home to find the wife he hadn't yet betrayed asleep in her sweatpants.

"I'll stop there," I said.

Returning to my seat, I peeked through the cracked door to confirm the safety and happiness of Byron. I flashed a thumbs-up at Abigail, who mouthed, *Thank you.* We made a good team.

It disturbed me that Simone and Ethan had chosen to sit next to each other. Her right knee touched his left beneath the table. My expectations, whatever they had been all those nights at Toady's, all those mornings waking up alone, were no longer accessible to me. If my manuscript was of the marriage-ending variety, would I not already know? Would my defense have been postponed for a family emergency?

Speaking of the family, I hadn't seen them jogging, or waiting in line for lattes, or strolling the quad with their beautiful heads ducked in private consultation. I'd passed their house and not a dahlia had stirred. Where had they been?

Simone adjusted the deep V of her blouse, and I knew the answer.

The first question came from Joyce. "As accomplished as the novel is, I can't help but wonder if the text relies too heavily on the sexualization of its characters. If these people were ordinary looking, or, God forbid, homely"—she pushed her tortoise-shell glasses up the bridge of her nose—"could the reader be expected to endure their melodrama? As the author embarks on her next project, I encourage her to think more deeply about her characters, especially the females of the story, for whom power too neatly translates to sex appeal."

Joyce turned the manuscript face down on the table. She scrunched her nose and hoped her critique did not betray her. Had she read more carefully, or with anything other than total indifference, she would have easily, swiftly decoded the name changes, the thinly disguised identifying details. As the department chair, it was Joyce's job to care when a lecturer and office staff member neglected to disclose their relation-ship, sexual in nature, to Human Resources. Or when a full professor emotionally, psychologically, and physically (if speed workouts count) abused a graduate student, leading to sleep deprivation, self-doubt, burnout, thoughts of academic fail-ure, and a touch of alcoholism. Punishments for rogue pro-fessors ranged from wrist slaps to forced sabbaticals—from a handful of anxiety-inducing meetings with the dean to stress levels incompatible with marriage. We'll never know what might have happened. The truth was, Joyce hadn't read past the first chapter of my thesis. Truthfully, she hadn't read a full thesis in ten years.

Ethan's concerns were thematic. "A novel covering such trod-upon ground as infidelity must have something new to say. There are moments in the text when Miss Green strikes upon real insight. The heroine's preoccupation with monogamy as an achievement to be included as such on her CV was, I thought, sharply observed."

Simone's hand went to rest on Ethan's thigh.

"At other times, Miss Green's plot points felt unearned or unmotivated. The infidelity itself was very abrupt, on my reading. For your next novel, consider specificity of conflict, and the inevitability of its resolution."

Abigail and I exchanged a glance. Come again, old man?

Finally, it was my advisor's turn to speak. I braced myself. The suspense was short-lived. Simone had no complaints. She heaped praise upon my manuscript. She called the novel riveting, at turns hilarious and heartbreaking, unflinching in its analysis of human ambivalence, and rigorously engaged with its influences, whom she cited as Barthes, Nabokov, Woolf, Barry Hannah, Richard Yates, Lorrie Moore, Lou Reed, for some reason Freud, and herself.

My disappointment was unlike anything I'd ever endured. My heart was an ice cream carton she had scraped clean with the sharp edge of her spoon. Simone turned away from my grief and wrote something at the top of the page in front of her.

"Now then," she said, covering the page with her forearm,

risking smeared ink on silk. "Does the candidate have any questions for her committee?"

Wouldn't you like to be loved by me?

I shook my head.

"If the candidate and her guest could step into the hall momentarily, the committee will reach a decision."

Leaving the room, I was not entirely without hope. What Simone wrote down was the approximate length of *I'm leaving him* or *You win.* The message I most wanted to receive from her was brief and straightforward, closed to interpretation, the opposite of a novel.

"Look at you!" Abigail gushed over her offspring, who sat cross-legged on a polished bench, playing a game in which he, a malevolent barber, gave unflattering haircuts to a series of clients who exited the screen in tears. At the sight of his mother, Byron yanked off his headphones and discarded the tablet, throwing his small arms around her soft midsection. "Mommy, I missed you!" *A performance of childhood,* I thought. Then corrected myself: a child.

In a year Abigail's father would die. His cancer would come back for him, and Diane would conceal the severity of the relapse until it was too late for Abigail to be of much use. The phone call came on a perfect spring day, not a cloud in the sky. Stepping orphaned into her dad's kitchen after leaving the hospital for the last time, Abigail would encounter Diane's forty-seven-year-old son, Franklin. He was stocky but trim. Well-groomed and symmetrical. His hair was nearly black. "Fuck," he said with unrestrained passion, laying eyes on Abigail's dewy beauty, her aura of beleaguered grief. "Thank God you're not my stepsister anymore." Franklin made good money in custom cabinetry. They were married on a boat in summer. The ringbearer's unauthorized speech concluded, "I hope you're all having an amazing life. I hope no one dies this year." The creative writing department's new administrative services coordinator was a forty-nine-year-old woman prone to prudery, platitudes, and smacking her gum. You get my point: Abigail lived happily ever after.

Leaning against the wall, sweating through my horrible blazer, I imagined Simone failing me. *Sorry, Robbie. Better luck next time.* I would write a new novel if she asked me to. I would beg her to show me how. Around the doorframe appeared Joyce's curls. "The candidate is invited back into the room." She giggled at her own formality. "Not you," she said to her dog sitter. "Just Roberta."

Now I stood before the judges. The three of them regarded me with amusement — or maybe I was projecting. Maybe they mostly wanted to get home and feed the cat, change into shorts, make it to Toady's in time for happy hour. Maybe I'd mistaken myself for the protagonist when I'd only ever been comic relief.

"Congratulations," Simone said.

Each of my committee members passed me a copy of their assessment, typed and printed and signed. At the top of Simone's, in her distinctive script: *Less is more.*

In her course Memory as Narrative, Simone had taught us to abandon our protagonists (ourselves) at the height of their emotions. Allow the narrator's eye to wander toward the window. Remark on a passing ice cream truck. It was useless to describe hearts pounding and sobs ricocheting; only in the absence of such description can the reader yield to the inevitable and—yes—begin to sob on their own.

Go ahead, I guess.

They took turns shaking my hand and enveloping me in hugs, chaste and slightly sweaty, as real people are. My intention was to leave the room and research the process for reporting a Title IX violation, and consider whether I had a case, whether I could win it, what winning would mean for me, and for Simone, and for my future as a person who hoped to love and be loved in return.

In the hall, Abigail packed up her maternal tote bag, and Ethan offered Byron a fist bump. Simone was already gone. Joyce could be heard making her way down the stairs, her voice directed into a phone but echoing off the marble. "Shish kebabs tonight, chicken *tomorrow*" was the last thing I ever heard her say. Grad school was over. I was in possession of a master's degree.

"Robbie," Ethan said. "Step into my office for a minute?"

He can't hurt me, I thought, before remembering the time he hit me with his car.

Inside his office, Ethan scribbled something on a sticky note. On his desk, between a stapler and a picture of Simone in Central Park, was a container of fresh figs. The truth of it hit me like a prison sentence: they were more each other's than ever. Ethan stuck the note to the tip of his finger and extended it toward me. "That's my agent's phone number. He's already read the book. He's a huge fan."

I wouldn't cry in front of Ethan.

"A 'once-in-a-generation talent' were his exact words. Thankfully we belong to different generations, or my ego would be permanently bruised."

We smiled foolishly at each other. I had no idea what he was thinking.

"Take care now," he said. "We're rooting for you."

ACKNOWLEDGMENTS

Thank you to Susan Ginsburg, my mentor, friend, and extraordinary agent. Thank you to Gaby Mongelli for the sharpest, smartest edits. I'm enormously grateful to everyone at Little, Brown and at Writers House, especially to Sally Kim, David Shelley, Catherine Bradshaw, Peyton Young, Alyssa Persons, Kayleigh George, Darcy Glastonbury, Arik Hardin, and Liz Hudson. Thank you so much to Jean Garnett.

Thank you to Justin Taylor and Rufi Thorpe for lifesaving notes and lifesaving friendship. Thank you to Kerry Winfrey, Alex Higley, Catherine Nichols, Carolyn Eyre, Adam Price, and Miranda Popkey. Thank you to all of ST.

Thank you to Dan for laughing. I love you.

Thank you to Sammy, Wes, and Ramona.

ABOUT THE AUTHOR

Emily Adrian is the author of *Daughterhood, The Second Season,* and *Everything Here Is Under Control,* as well as two critically acclaimed novels for young adults. Her work has appeared in *Granta, Joyland, The Point, EPOCH, Alta Journal,* and *Los Angeles Review of Books.* Originally from Portland, Oregon, Adrian currently lives in New Haven, Connecticut.